I0663742

The People's

Republic

of

47th and Long

S.W. Campbell

Published by Shawn Campbell

The People's Republic of 47th and Long

ISBN: 978-1-7332314-8-0

To Chris the bus driver, the nicest man I ever met.
The good ones always go too soon.

The People's Republic of 47th and Long

April 22, 2022

Dear Friends,

Happy Friday to you from the People's Republic of 47th and Long. I hope that this bright day brings you warmth and comfort in your home across the Great River. We hear rumors of what is happening up there, but little reliable since the bridges came down last month. It is likely for the best. I never trusted those blue uniformed TSA goons to keep people from crossing the 205 as was promised, and well, you know my opinion on the refuse that remains on Hayden Island. No, though it takes longer for my letters to reach you now, I think we are all better off with a little bit more distance between us.

Today was a glorious day for our little experiment, for our dear Jon Seabreeze, accredited accountant, peacefully annexed the Johnson household on the corner of 52nd and Raymond, marking the first time our little experiment has managed to cross the four lanes of 52nd into the territory claimed without merit by the Foster-Powell Neighborhood Association. Oh, they may claim that such territory belongs to them, but if it were true then the Johnson's would not be coming to us for protection from the rampant degradations of the Survivors who still plague the area. I doubt that the powers that be in the Foster-Powell Neighborhood Association will do much about it beyond creating a committee to discuss the possibility of debating whether or not they should do something. Thank god I live in a place of action here beneath the Japanese maple flag.

I received a letter the other day from Mom and Charlie. They're of course still living out in the wilds. I have offered to vouch for their cleanliness if they wished to come to live with me, but of course they refused as always. They are like so many still living out there, still convinced that the magic Cheetoh will somehow come back to life, and everything will be the same as it once was. Silly I know. Still holding on for dear life to a world that is dead and gone. No magic Cheetoh can bring any of it back. Mom of course writes as though things are much the same there as they always have been, as long as one doesn't venture far from home. I hear whole swaths east of the mountains are controlled by Survivors.

Anyways, that is all the news I know. I hope you managed to get whatever it was getting into your veggie patch. Give my best to Danny.

Your friend,
Leopold

April 26, 2022

Dear Friends,

I greatly enjoyed your recent letter. The description of your battle with the raccoon was most entertaining. We don't seem to have any issues with raccoons here anymore. Jon Seabreeze put us to clearing them out last season, which proved prudent as we had little loss and good stores for the winter. I don't know how it is up there, but here you can't always trust in the Safeway trucks coming as they say they will. Plus, people always crowd when they do arrive, which still makes me nervous. Rumors of new outbreaks always abound. I heard the other day that an explosion of new cases erupted down in Gladstone, and now everyone is afraid to go outside again there. I don't know who's running things on your side of the Great River these days, but it might be good to suggest a campaign to cull raccoons and other such pests. You know, just to be safe.

Besides, even without the threat of the virus, things are getting a little more dicey when it comes to the trucks. Too many different groups coming together in one spot. You can tell there's going to be trouble some day. A few times things have gotten close, and the driver has warned they'll stop deliveries if things ever get out of hand. The contingent we send from the People's Republic are always on their best behavior, but the Bernie Boys from Brentwood and the Warrenites down at Reed College can't seem to help themselves. They got into a big scuffle down by the old Lutz Tavern the other day. Left several on both sides pretty bloody. Bad deal all around. I for one would prefer to keep the peace. Jon Seabreeze says it's better to absorb rather than to attack, and I for one agree with him. He's one smart cookie. Just this week three more households joined up on Cora Street. Things are definitely going well. On some streets, you wouldn't even know anything has changed from what my Mom keeps referring to as normal.

Speaking of such things, Mom hasn't written to me lately. I think she's having a bit of a snit with me because I called her naive in my last letter. I don't know what she expects from me. She used to never be a big fan of the Cheetoh, but now I'm willing to bet she's one of those with his picture hanging in the house. Given all the shit he did, I don't really understand it, but maybe nostalgia tends to dull the edges. In some ways I guess we should be grateful. After all, without him we would've never had this opportunity to build a better world.

Take care of yourself and tell Danny to put some lotion on that rash if he can find any.

Your friend,
Leopold.

April 30, 2022

Dear Friends,

The Safeway truck didn't come this week. God only knows what happened to it. After all, Boise is a long ways away. I'm willing to bet if something happened, it probably happened around Troutdale. That entire area is nothing but Survivors by as far as I can tell. Oh, I'm sure there's still some people cowering in their homes, but who wants to just sit around until those thugs bust in to spit in your mouths? No thank you. Thank god Jon Seabreeze makes sure we set patrols. If only those idiots at the Foster-Powell Neighborhood Association would do the same. They pretty much let anyone walk across their territory as much as they please. Is it any wonder then why another two households east of 52nd joined us in just the past few days.

We had a bit of a strange happening here the other day. A group of Essentials came right down Holgate. You should have seen them, sweating in their plastic suits and taking notes on clipboards. They must have been a part of some different group of Essentials than those who carry the mail, because they sure as hell didn't report for disinfection before crossing the line into the People's Republic. Gary Gunderson took a few of the younger members of the patrol out to meet them. Even took a couple of pistols to really show they meant business. It kind of reminded me of back in the early days, when the Japanese maple flag only flew over a couple of blocks and we still had joggers and other such wanderers crossing anywhere they pleased, before we stopped them.

5

Anyways, these Essentials claimed they were looking into the possibility of stringing back up some of the electric lines down Holgate. We all had a pretty good laugh at their expense. How long do they think such things would stay up before the Survivors ripped them down again? Lack of pattern recognition I guess. Either way, we sent them back the way they came. Last thing we need is a bunch of strangers tracking in anything. Their leader tried to bring up the same old rigmarole about vaccinations and the such, but we ignored her. Guess you have to respect their optimism. Kind of reminded me of Mom a bit.

Hope the heavy rain over the past few days helps your garden. Don't forget what I said about the racoons. A little leadership in these times is never a bad thing. Also, tell Danny he's going to need to do better than puns if he wants to make people laugh.

Your friend,
Leopold

May 8, 2022

Dear Friends,

Things I miss in the world:
1. Hot showers (though I guess I should be glad the Essentials keep the water going).
2. Eating at restaurants.
3. Toilet paper.
4. Pornography.

If I can be straight-forward with you, which I think by our years of friendship I can, I wish to god every time we absorb another household that it's gonna be one with a single lady, but of course I hardly ever have such luck. I guess it's what I get for moving into a family neighborhood all those years ago, but of course back then I thought that maybe by now I'd have a family. Oh sure, sometimes maybe somebody gives me the eye, but I can tell you already that such things are likely to be nothing but trouble. There was a fella who used to live next door to me named David who got himself hooked by such a wandering eye once. Jon Seabreeze had to send him away, because we already have enough going against us without dividing ourselves. I hear up in some of the old apartment complexes there's Survivors or other such folk who do things for you in return for supplies, but of course I'd never do such a thing. How could I ever put my own needs before that of the Republic? No sir, we are building a better world here.

I made just such a mistake back when everything was just beginning, back when we had no idea where everything was headed. They had just issued the stay at home orders, but I drove into Washington County to get a little something something, even though that's where all the cases early on were popping up. Of course at that time most of us really didn't take any of that flattening the curve stuff that seriously. The person I met got sick soon after, caught it from some chump at her work, but luckily I never did. Still though, can you imagine how guilty I would've felt if anybody got it from me? Quarantined myself for two weeks, never even a single symptom. Lucky son of a bitch I guess.

Nothing much to report around here. Vegetable patches are looking good and a new Safeway truck made it through. Still no word on what happened to the last one. Maybe they just never sent it. Don't know what we would do if that was the case. Tell Danny that rash will never clear up if he doesn't stop picking at it.

You're friend,
Leopold

May 10, 2022

Dear Friends,

The Brentwood Bernie Boys went into old Eastmoreland this evening and started burning fancy rich people houses again. Not sure why they bother, given pretty much all of those houses have been empty for the past year, but maybe I'm just not as young and full of pep as I used to be. Many of us climbed up on our roofs from which we could see the flames. The Warrenites must have retaliated from Reed because we heard a few scattered warning shots, but I don't think it was much of a dustup, otherwise we would've heard more of a racket. Either way, I'm betting maybe a dozen houses or so got burned.

While I was up on the roof I looked towards downtown a bit. Looking at that old familiar skyline tucked beneath the West Hills it was almost possible to imagine things like they used to be, at least until one noticed all the windows in Big Pink and most of the other buildings are busted out. It seems so strange to think that it wasn't that long ago that all of us used to go there every day. It's only been what, two years since that was our normal, but it feels like a lifetime ago. I wonder what things are like there now. I haven't been there since just after the riots. I was curious so I took my bike down to see. Lots of broken and boarded up windows, graffiti, and burned out cars. Not sure if anyone is still living down there. Can't imagine even the hobos sticking around these days. I didn't stay too long. I wasn't supposed to have gone out that far.

Mom got over being cranky with me long enough to write, or maybe I just wasn't patient enough. I always forget how long it takes letters to get all the way over the mountains and back. Apparently, a small group of Survivors beat up a couple of people living on the edge of town. The Turtles hunted them down, lined them up against a wall, and shot them. The Turtles don't take any crap out there, which Mom thinks is a good thing. She thinks I should find a way to come out there to them. Thinks it will be safer until things get back to normal. I'm of course not going to do it. I can't see how living in a place where the Turtles get to shoot anyone they want is any safer than here. No, I think I'd rather be on the cusp of some brighter new future, not desperately holding on to whatever is left of the old. I guess I can't blame Mom for feeling different about such things. It's harder to adapt when you're old. I've always wondered what Charlie thinks about all of it.

Well, that's most of what's been going on. Lots of excitement, so now you get two letters instead of one. Pretty good deal. Hope Danny's rash is getting better and hope everyone is doing well.

Your friend,
Leopold

May 15, 2022

Hello Friends:

Do you remember that Nurse Nancy who used to live not that far
from me? The one with the thick black braid who Danny dated
for like a hot minute before she wised up and dumped his ass?
No offense Danny, but you had a pattern for a bit there. I don't
know. I used to see her around every now and again. You
know, at the grocery store or something like that. One time I
saw her down at the hardware store and she was buying this big
bag of nails, and all I could think to myself was what in the hell
is she going to do with that big bag of nails? I mean it was big.
She must have been buying several pounds worth. They had to
go into the back to get another box. They tried to talk her into
buying the whole box, but she just wouldn't do it. She insisted
they had to be in the bag. Who does something like that? Who
gets so stubborn that they insist on doing something even though
it makes better sense to do something else?

I remember when things started to fall apart, it never seemed to
matter to her. She left every morning at daybreak and went to
the Providence down in Milwaukie, then came back every
evening in the dark. She must have been working over twelve
hour shifts, almost every day. Just stubborn I guess. Hell, even
too stubborn to get sick apparently, though pretty much every
Essential who worked in the hospitals got it eventually. Most
pretty bad. Virus load you know. No idea how she never got
sick. We were all expecting it, everyone in the neighborhood
that is. Every other Essential seemed to be getting sick. It's just
what happened. There was never enough protective gear back

then. They were pretty much down to trash bags near the end, but she never got sick. It doesn't make any sense. Just none of it made a damn bit of sense. Woman like that, I guess Danny should feel lucky she broke up with him.

Through it all I used to always wonder about those nails. Why in the hell was she buying so many damn nails. I did eventually find out. I can remember going into her house back when Jon Seabreeze was just getting things really started. There wasn't much there, not a lot of furniture or anything. The kind of house owned by a workaholic. Just a place to sleep, nothing much more. Except for there was this big old piece of plywood leaned up against one wall in what should've been the dining room if she had a table. It had nails of all sizes and colors driven into it. You should've seen it. She was making a mosaic out of nails. It was about three-quarters of the way done. It was this horse running across a meadow, with a line of trees in the background and a big storm coming. It was really something. Anyways, I don't know why I'm writing to you about that. Just popped in my head and felt the need to write it down. No use burning perfectly good paper, so decided might as well send it. Give Danny my best.

Leopold

May 19, 2022

Dear Friends:

It's a glorious day today in the People's Republic of 47th and Long. Jon Seabreeze, with the help of Gary Gunderson, convinced fifteen new households to join us up by Creston Park, effectively fully absorbing that area. While there are still a few households here and there who remain unaffiliated, I'm sure it won't be long until they realize the benefits being offered to them. Not counting the random collection of houses sticking out here or there, this brings our borders roughly in line with 39th, Powell, 52nd, and Harold. If my calculations are correct this brings our little country to right around 180 hectares, that's right we're converting to the metric system, and 2,200 people. Not too bad for a brand new country if I might say so myself. After all, Vatican City is only 49 hectares, and nobody has ever questioned whether or not it's a country. I had Linda, the one who makes the bread, look it up in her World Books for me. Crazy what Boomers still have isn't it.

This isn't the first bit of expansionist news this week either. Earlier this week a couple more houses on the other side of 52nd agreed to join, no doubt convinced by how pleased the Johnsons seem with their choice to join. It's hard to believe sometimes how fast we're growing. At this rate we'll have doubled in size again by this time next year. Crazy to think it all started with Jon Seabreeze going door to door in the neighborhood, asking if we could all agree to designate seven to eight in the morning as a time where just Boomers could walk around so they could get out of their houses. Now look at us, well on our way to really creating something new and better.

Sorry, I know it's not your favorite when I start going on and on about such things, but it's hard not to be proud, especially for us who have been a part of it since the beginning. We've built something here, and it's catching on. It's hard not to be proud of it.

Did you ever get that raccoon problem taken care of? If not, maybe it's time to start thinking more about the future. We've had great success here, and there's no reason it couldn't be replicated up in your neck of the woods. Some people might talk about the end of the world as we know it, but down here we talk about new beginnings. If I had to choose between the two, I know which one I'd choose. Anyways, take care. Tell Danny I thought about that time we got drunk and he puked down the side of the Uber guy's car. Had a good laugh.

Your Friend,
Leopold

May 22, 2022

Hello Friends:

I helped at the school today, overseeing some of the younger kids while they worked in the garden, mostly pulling weeds and the such. I'll say this for our new curriculum, it's certainly more hands on than we got when we were kids. More practical in many ways. I imagine this will probably be for the best. Of course, this is not to say that we're raising a next generation of practical idiots. No, they still get the usual rounds of reading, writing, arithmetic, etc.; just everything is more adapted to real world uses. We're all pretty proud of our school here.

While I was helping, some of the kids got started talking about how things used to be, with the old Oaks Bottom amusement park being an especial focus for whatever reason. Generally, we discourage the kids from reminiscing too much about the old world, but I let them go on for a while, because to be honest, it was kind of nice to travel back with them. Do you remember when we used to get drunk and ride on the rollercoaster? I was always too big for it so my knees would always get banged up, but it was still pretty fun. Remember watching the roller derby girls? That seems like something that would be fairly easy to bring back, if we could find the roller skates. I wonder how many people might have roller skates tucked away somewhere. Anyways, now here I am reminiscing too much.

I got your letter from a week ago recently. It seems like we're cursed to just keep missing each other, always a letter or two ahead. Either way, it's always nice to hear from you. It sounds like you guys are getting a little more organized up there, which is good, but I would caution against falling into the same mistakes as the Foster-Powell Neighborhood Association. Too many cooks in the kitchen spoils the broth as they say, and too much looking back keeps you from going forward. It's amazing the things that can get done with a little effective organization. Thank god we have it down here. I'd hate to imagine living elsewhere.

Not too much else to say right now I guess. It's amazing how nice the weather has been of late, though it would be nice to have a bit more rain so we don't have to use the spinklers too much. Water still comes out of the pipes, but like the Safeway trucks, I don't think we want to stay too reliant on them. God only knows how long such things might last. We're looking into maybe digging a well, but we don't really have anybody with much expertise in that kind of thing. Either way, the more we can sustain ourselves the better. It would also be nice if we could get our hands on some goats or something. Anyways, give my best to Danny.

Your friend,
Leopold

May 26, 2022

Dear Friends,

They have me walking the perimeter at night now. I have been helping rip up pavement along 48th in order to clear more ground for gardens, which is necessary but back breaking work, so the change in pace is nice. From dark until dawn I walk the border of the Republic with around forty others, plus another ten moving around on bikes. Each of us carry some kind of club, I have a baseball bat, and a whistle so we can call for help if needed. It takes maybe an hour to walk the whole perimeter. I used to do such things in the early days, but of course back then it wasn't such a long walk.

It was kind of exciting to be out at night. Wandering the streets, you can almost imagine that it is just a normal quiet evening like any evening from years past. It always amazes me how many stars you can see now that the light pollution is pretty much gone. The whole swath of the Milky Way was above my head. God it makes you feel small. Is it any wonder we became so arrogant when we never got a chance to revel in exactly how small we actually are? Of course, I don't have much time for philosophizing. Night patrol is an important job. Last thing we need is for some Survivors sneaking in to run amok because I was too busy gaping at the night sky. I don't know. I know that clearing ground and tending gardens is important work, maybe the most important work, but I'll admit that patrolling strangely fills me with a greater sense of accomplishment. Maybe it's because of the personal risk.

It's a little nerve wracking being out by yourself in the middle of the night. We're all at least a couple of blocks apart when we're making our circuits. Several of the houses on the edge are inhabited still, though many aren't. It's interesting when we absorb new areas to see which people move to empty houses deeper inside and which ones are more stubborn and want to take the risk. A lot of people, especially the new ones, still have a lot of sense of ownership over such things. Kind of silly I think, but change takes time.

Nothing of note really happened. I did hear some noises several times, but they all turned out to be just the wind and once a possum. I was a bit jumpy when I first started out but got pretty used to everything by the end. Except the possum of course, there's something about them that creeps the shit out of me. That big mouth full of teeth maybe. Anyways, I think I'm going to take a nap since I'm going to be patrolling again tonight. Tell Danny he needs to start washing his clothes more or something. That rash sounds like it's getting worse.

Your Friend,
Leopold

May 31, 2022

Dear Friends:

I met a man last night while out on patrol up in the recently annexed area in the northeast. He was sitting on his porch, smoking a joint, and he called me a mom fucker when I walked by, but apologized when I stopped to talk with him. I didn't take it personally. A lot of these recently independent households are that way, especially anymore given they've been surviving on their own for quite a while. There's a certain amount of pride that comes with such things, and I imagine it's a bit of blow when they're forced to realize they have no other options. I don't know. Maybe I'm just spit balling on this one. The thought of going it on my own never even crossed my mind. After all, no man is an island.

At the least this guy seemed the decent sort. He seemed more tired than mad, a man who had fought long and hard only to lose. His name was Darin Greene and apparently he used to be some mid-manager at Nike in the soccer department or something like that, or maybe it was football, the American type that is. I don't know, I tend not to listen too much when people start going on about their old lives. Such things aren't that important unless your old job gave you some useful skills, which mid-manager usually doesn't. Most of them seem to end up doing grunt work of one type or another, and to be honest, most seem happier with the fact that nobody is looking to them to run things anymore, though maybe I'm just being biased.

Anyways, Darin Greene shared some of his joint with me, he must grow some of his own or something, which was a bit of a treat. Haven't smoked any in well over a year. Gave me a bit of a light step for a little while at least. Kind of reminded me of the Oscar parties we used to have. Oh, don't get me wrong, I probably shouldn't have done it, but you know, I'm only human. It's kind of like getting nips from the distillers every now and again. We all know the score, we need the ethanol for disinfectant, but it's nice to get just a rare taste every now and again. I imagine things will be better with the next generation. For them not having such things will just be normal. Probably for the best.

I didn't tell Mr. Greene that he better enjoy his joints while he had them. He had enough of a chip on his shoulder as it was, and he'd find out soon enough anyways. They usually give the newbies a little bit of time to adjust, but the growing season is only so long, and we can't afford to be wasting space. Hope you and Danny are doing well.

Cheers,
Leopold

June 2, 2022

Hello Again Friends,

I was thinking the other day about how I used to go running through Reed College, down on the trails along the lake. I remember one of the last times I ran there, back during the first stay at home order. I went down Woodstock and then turned up into the campus. There were a bunch of students there even though the school was shut down, doing an impromptu graduation ceremony. They were all in dresses, button down shirts, and a few random jumpers for some reason, must have been the new style or something, wearing wreaths around their heads as though they had just won the ancient Olympics. Most were in clumps, definitely not six feet apart. They made their own speeches and sprayed champagne on each other, screaming with the excitement of youth, imagining this point in their lives as some kind of high point. For some it probably was. I remember a little ways away an older man was talking to a groundskeeper, angrily gesturing towards the gathering. The groundskeeper just shrugged his shoulders in that way people do when they feel like there is nothing they can do.

Selfish little bastards. Though I guess almost all of us are selfish at that age, especially when we've been raised in a world of privilege where the biggest worries are of one's own psychology. They were so cocky in their youth, thinking it a shield, none of us at the time knowing that the second wave would be so much less discerning. I imagine some of them were the same ones who rioted when they tried to turn all the college dormitories into hospitals and quarantine centers. God the foolishness of it all.

I guess I shouldn't judge too harshly. I remember just prior to the first stay at home orders, when everybody still thought not gathering in groups of twenty-five or more was a hardship. I was helping an old woman write and publish her memoirs and we were supposed to have our last meeting to go over the proof. I didn't want to go, but she insisted. She told me she lived alone, was ninety, was in hospice, and probably had less than six months to live. She wanted to get the memoir done, so I went. It was right after I left that I got the call that I had been exposed. I always felt guilty about it. She of course died, though of cancer, but it could have easily been different. After all, pretty much all of the Greats died in the end.

Do you remember the time Danny got real drunk that one night and followed that stray dog around the park, peeing everywhere it did? That was pretty funny.

Take care of yourselves.

Leopold

June 4, 2022

Dear Friends,

You're going to get so many letters in one go you're not going to know what to do with them. LOL. I guess that's not really all that of a bad thing. I spent most of today helping in the gardens, mostly weeding since I don't have that much of a green thumb. It's strangely relaxing. When I was a kid, I used to hate gardening. Mom had a giant garden, and I would often have to help with the weeding, often as a punishment for being a pain in the ass one way or another. I guess it might have soured me on the whole thing, because I didn't even go near a garden again for years. Now the feeling of the earth on my hands brings up nothing but warm remembrances. It's funny how the world works.

Sometimes in the evening, Charlie would go out amongst the potato plants to pick off the potato bugs, big black and yellow striped bastards, not to be confused with what we used to always call pill bugs, or roly-polys as some people call them. He'd carry with him an old oil pint, with just a bit of oil still in the bottom and drop the bugs into it. He'd then screw on the cap and give it a shake. One time he let me look into it and it had what seemed like thousands of them in it. The smell of all of them dying was terrible. A musty smell with a sharp pungency. Looking into that bottle would make my skin crawl, but still, I'd always look. My Mom would often help comb the potato leaves for them, but I could never get myself to do it. Even now I have to force myself to pick up a bug.

Joanna Seabreeze came out to help us weed for a while. She's always out in the gardens whenever possible, her skin kissed by the sun and her head protected by a handkerchief. Mrs. Seabreeze knows a lot about gardens. She used to run a garden supply shop so long ago. She whispers to the plants while she works, encouraging them to grow big and strong, promising that she'll take care of them and thanking them for helping us. If she catches you watching her doing such things, she never looks embarrassed, she just gives you a knowing smile as though the two of you have a mutual understanding of the secrets of the world. You hardly ever see Jon Seabreeze in the gardens, other than inspections so he always knows what's going on, but sometimes his wife will ask him to help her with something, and he will bend down into the dirt and follow her every direction as amicably as a loving child.

We got several days of rain here last week. The vegetables seemed glad to have it. I'll be tired tonight with all this work, but I know I'll fall asleep happy. Give Danny my best.

Your friend,
Leopold

June 9, 2022

Dear Friends,

Sometimes you just wake up in a funk. That's the way things were in the old world, and no matter what wonders we create, at times it is the way things are going to be in the new. These are the hard mornings. The mornings where it seems like everything you do is pointless and you just want to stay in bed, curled up in a ball to protect your interior bits from the horrors of the outside world. It's the time when the full weight of everything seems to be pressing itself downward. They are the times that we feel the most naked and alone. These are not the times to despair. These are the times to force ourselves forward. These are the times we must set small attainable goals and work towards them. These are the times to share our burdens, not shoulder them alone. The path is dark and long, but don't worry friends, we all walk it together.

A group of Survivors came up to the boundary yesterday. There were maybe twenty of them, all on bikes. It was midday. Maybe they hoped to sneak in unnoticed, which seems unlikely, or maybe they just wanted to scare us. Either way, within minutes of them being spotted whistles were blown and a crowd of us came out to meet them. They were a rough looking bunch. Matted hair and clothes turning the grayish brown of never being washed. They came down Harold Street, territory claimed by the Foster-Powell Neighborhood Association, unmolested and acting like they owned the place. We met them at 52nd and refused to let them come any further. Some rode their bikes back and forth, screaming jeers and threats, trying to get themselves amped up for god only knows what, but none dared cross the center line. We mostly did nothing, at least until they started spitting at us, which though ineffective raised the blood enough on our side that Gary Gunderson decided it was time to put a stop to such things. He shot a 22 round over their heads and made it apparent the next one would be aimed lower. The Survivors retreated back up Harold.

I was there when Gary told Jon Seabreeze about it. You could tell both were angry. For all its grandiose claims, the Foster-Powell Neighborhood Association is little more than falsehoods and bravado. How can they be letting Survivors cross their territory, in the middle of the fucking day no less? Do they care nothing for their neighbors, never mind their own people? It's frightening to think about. We're probably going to have to put more people on patrols. That's going to slow down some of the other projects, important projects, but our first duty is to protect what we have created. Those fucking Survivors are nuts. God only knows what they'd do if we let them. I hope you and Danny are staying safe.

Your friend,
Leopold

June 12, 2022

Dear Friends,

It's finally been decided that we should build cisterns to collect rainwater for later use, the well idea has been abandoned as unfeasible. Nobody in the Republic has any experience digging wells, we have none of the needed tools, and we have no idea how deep we'd have to go. I've heard before that bedrock is at about twenty feet around here, which I imagine means we'd have to go deeper than that, through rock. I don't know. Either way, the idea has been abandoned, which seems like the most prudent thing to do. As I've been saying for months, we live in a god damn place where it rains like a gajillion inches every year. It doesn't make any sense for us to waste it, especially given that we have no idea when we might lose water. I know the Essentials have been keeping it flowing and that the pipes are underground so it's hard for the Survivors to get at them, but still, as Jon Seabreeze always says, you just never know, so it's better to be prepared. After all, just two years ago who would have thought we'd be without electricity and phones?

To be honest, the whole thing irks me quite a bit. I said from the very beginning that the well was a stupid idea and that we should be building cisterns, though in politer terms of course, and now we've wasted weeks that could've been put to better use. But of course, Smiley Dave Larson was for a well, so we ended up doing that instead, all because he's a likable asshole who could start a conversation with a tree. Maybe I'm being too harsh. Dave isn't stupid, he just latches onto things before fully thinking them through, and once he latches on it becomes his idea and it's hard to get him to even consider alternatives. Of course, he was the one who brought up cisterns again once it became too obvious that digging a well wasn't going to work, so of course now he's getting all the credit as though it was his original idea. I guess I shouldn't complain. After all, we are getting the cisterns.

It's not going to be easy to build them. Concrete is of course hard to come by, though there might still be some left in the old hardware store or Bi-Mart down on Woodstock. Can't imagine the Survivors or Bernie Boys having much use for it. We can always come up with alternative solutions if needed. Like most things it will probably end up a mishmash of about every idea you can think of.

I haven't heard from Mom in a while. I think maybe she's actually having a bit of a fit this time since I told her I had no interest in coming back, but maybe not. It worries me. Tell Danny hi.

Your friend,
Leopold

June 20, 2022

Dear Friends:

Sorry for the delay in writing to you, but I've been very busy of late with my patrol duties. Gangs of survivors have been appearing with increasing frequency and Gary has us patrolling shifts and a half in order to have more people walking the boundary at all times. They don't want to put more people on patrol because they're trying to move forward as quickly as possible with the gardening and building cisterns. The Bernie Boys and Warrenites almost got into a fight at the last Safeway truck drop off and the driver got onto his microphone and warned that any violence would result in the drop off spot being declared unsafe. Idiots. Suffice to say everyone is pretty well on edge.

Over the past week, groups of Survivors have shown up to the perimeter three times, usually in the early morning or late evening. The second time was a big group of around thirty, but the other two were small groups of around fifteen on bikes. We spotted them quickly enough each time, and they always left without trying anything beyond screaming obscenities and spitting at us from the other side of the street, but still worrisome. Especially given that they seem to be different groups, not the same one coming again and again.

The most worrisome thing about all of it is the fact that they keep coming at us through the Foster-Powell Neighborhood Association. Gary seems convinced that they're letting Survivor groups through to punish us for annexing households east of

52nd, but I'm not so sure. Those Foster-Powell idiots have never been the best at securing their boundaries against Survivor incursions, its half the reason households keep abandoning them to join us. As Charlie always says: "though not a hard rule, incompetence tends to be the more likely answer." I don't know. Either way, you can tell that Jon Seabreeze is very concerned about it. He's spending more time with his wife in the gardens, something he tends to do when he really needs to think about something.

I'm becoming very concerned about Mom. I still haven't heard from her and it's unusual for her to be cranky about things for this long. God only knows what might happen over the mountains between all the Survivors and Turtles over there. I'd hate to think something happened, so I just keep telling myself I'm being silly, and everything is okay. I wrote a letter to her and Charlie a few days ago, so hopefully I hear back from them soon. This is not the time to go off on a snit. I'm glad you are all staying safe on your side of the Great River.

Your friend,
Leopold

June 21, 2022

Hello Friends:

I'm having trouble sleeping this morning, so I'm trying writing to see if it will help. I guess this means you get two letters in one go. I had a very vivid and strange dream, a literal kaleidoscope of flashing nonsensical images which assaulted my brain from every possible angle. I was standing in a garden which flowed around ivy covered houses like a verdant green ocean softly shuffling in the breeze. It stretched as far as the eye could see, but nobody was there but me. The vegetables were prime for picking, but as it was only me, I could not keep up as they grew before my very eyes in an ever rising bounty promising safety and security if I just could keep up with it. I worked in a frenzy, sweat stinging my eyes until in an instant it was all gone, replaced by a meadow with a distant line of trees and mountains. A horse was running across the meadow at full tilt, a beautiful roan rushing away from a fire in the trees, its mane and tail sheltering smoking embers. It ran past me as though I didn't even exist, and I turned away from the flaming trees to watch it go. Then there was nothing, an empty world of nothing.

These night patrols have my sleep schedule all sorts of screwed up, especially on my days off. I try to help out around the Republic as much as possible, but sometimes I sleep during the morning and sometimes during the afternoon. I seem to be the most awake right now in the early morning for some reason, before most people have roused themselves from bed. I like to climb up on my roof and look out at the world. Sometimes I look towards the mountains, wondering about Mom, but other times I look towards downtown and think about back when daily trips there were the norm. I imagine myself driving down Holgate, staring upwards at the red and white radio tower standing proud in the West Hills. Then I see the metal stumps where the tower once stood, and I fall back into reality and remember the mantra that we must always follow. We must go forward. This is an opportunity to make things better.

I'm probably being overly gloomy. It's often nice up on the roof. It's peaceful to watch the world slowly come awake. To hear the first songs of the morning birds and note the early risers as they begin their days. It would be nice to sip some tea while up on the roof, but it wouldn't be right to waste the wood on such frivolities. It's our duty to minimize wood use as much as possible. Wood trucks are so much more rare than Safeway trucks. I wonder why the Essentials turned off the gas but kept the water going? All the pipes are underground. Who knows? Just one more thing we'll need to figure out I guess. At least the winters are never really all that cold, at least compared to so many other places. Anyways, I'm rambling.

Your friend,
Leopold

June 27, 2022

Dear Friends:

An airplane flew over today, a single prop model that made quite
a racket. I can't remember the last time a plane flew over, but
it's definitely been a while. Everybody got kind of excited about
it. Everybody was looking up. It was pretty high up. Some of
the kids ran around with their arms outstretched, making plane
noises. It kind of had a weird effect. People started talking
about how things used to be and speculating about what it might
be doing up there. My guess is Essentials doing something.
Essentials are always up to something that will never work, but
they like to stay busy. Who knows. It flew around fifteen
minutes or so and then headed south. After that people got back
to work. A couple people still talked about it, but it was largely
forgotten by the end of the day.

We had a bit of excitement a few nights ago. Survivors showed
up again, this time in the middle of the night. This time they
came up Steele, ballsy as could be. There were maybe ten of
them, though it was hard to tell in the dark. I was maybe eight
blocks away when I heard the whistles, so I rushed to help face
them. I had just arrived when I heard more whistles, up by
Center, and then more down by 42nd. There were small groups
it seemed like everywhere. Half the ones we were watching split
off and disappeared back into the night. Whistles kept sounding
and nobody seemed to know what to do. They'd appear in one
place, just to retreat back out of sight and pop up again
somewhere else. This went on for a bit, and then things got
really bad. A couple gunshots went off and then the bike patrols

started sounding their airhorns, which is never a good
thing. Airhorns means the boundary has been breached and
anyone who is able to get up and help needs to get their ass in
gear. It's been a while since the airhorns have gone off. The
Survivors ran away into the night, but it got people pretty riled
up.

Jon Seabreeze and everyone else seem pretty convinced that the
Foster-Powell Neighborhood Association is letting the Survivors
through on purpose. I don't know if I'm quite convinced, but
either way, it's getting out of hand and something needs to be
done. We're going to be sending a delegation over to talk to
them. Good old Smiley Dave Larson was chosen to lead it, and
for whatever reason he asked for me to go too. I guess I should
be complemented. It is quite an honor to represent the Republic,
though I'm not looking forward to being in quarantine for two
weeks when I get back. Those bastards in Foster-Powell are
probably crawling with virus. Be the first time outside since I
went on that long bike trip to scout around. I'll of course go,
after all, my community needs me. Hope you and Danny are
well.

Your friend,
Leopold

July 2, 2022

Hello Friends,

Sorry for not writing for a bit, but as you can probably imagine things have been rather busy. I'm in quarantine now so if I get sick you'll never see this letter, but I figured I might as well write anyways, it's not like there's a hell of a lot else to do shut up like this. The quarantine house I'm in is actually the house next to mine. My neighbor was an Essential, a police officer. It's kind of strange to be in because all the houses on my block were all built around the same time and in the same style, all 1950's bungalows, and this one is a perfect mirror image of mine, so it's kind of like I'm living in a backwards world right now. I keep turning in the wrong direction to get to things and at night I've bumped into the wall a couple of times trying to get to the bathroom. After two weeks of this I'll probably get used to it enough where it will screw me up when I'm back home.

It's not bad here, though a bit boring. The Republic has about five of these quarantine houses now, and they're pretty well set up. All the flooring is linoleum and the paint on the walls is all high gloss, so pretty easy to clean. Most of the furniture is plastic patio furniture, even the bed which is actually a lounger. About the only things in here that would be a bitch to clean are the blankets and the couple of books they let me bring in with me, though I guess all of it could be easily burned if needed. Knocking on wood it won't come to that, you know, given what that would mean.

I can't complain too much. I don't like being in here obviously, butI was glad to be able to help serve the Republic in such an important capacity. I think the meeting with the Foster-Powell Neighborhood Association went fairly well, though Smiley Dave Larson would probably call it more of a great success, but to him everything is a great success so you always have to take his opinions with a bit of cynic salt. It was interesting to see how other people are doing things, and I'll tell you what, it really made me feel lucky that I live in the People's Republic of 47th and Long. It's kind of frightening to think that if I had bought a house elsewhere all those years ago how different my life might be. Just dumb luck of course, but still, it's funny the things that turn out to be important.

I'll have to tell you about it more later. Getting a bit tired now. I will say that getting out of the Republic a bit did make me worry about you guys more. I hope everything is okay. I'm also worried about Mom and Charlie. Still haven't heard a peep from them.

Yours Truly,
Leopold

July 3, 2022

Hello Friends,

It was a strange thing to cross the street into the Foster-Powell Neighborhood Association. I'll be the first to admit that it scared me a bit. It's only a patch of pavement dividing us, but what a difference that divide makes. I guess the first thing I noticed was that things seemed less orderly. Oh sure, they had their gardens and the rest just like us, but they weren't organized gardens, instead it seemed as though each household was doing its own thing. The second thing I noticed was that many of the trees have been cut down. I've looked across many times and never noticed it before. The People's Republic is a veritable forest in comparison. I said it once, and I'll say it again, thank god for whatever strange twist of geographic fate landed me in buying a house where I did.

The meeting was perhaps the most frightening part of all of it. They held it in the old union hall on Foster. I think Smiley Dave and I expected to be just meeting a few members of their leadership, but no, they had other ideas. They packed the damn place full. There must have been a couple hundred people crammed inside. Can you believe the insanity? That many people in close quarters? Inside? What could they be thinking? I started sweating the moment I sat down. I tried my best not to touch anything. Thank god I was just there for support and Smiley Dave did most of the talking. I'm not much of a public speaker anyways, and I certainly couldn't have done well with that crowd loudly reacting to everything said.

To be honest, I had a little trouble focusing on the meeting itself. It seemed like Smiley Dave was having to debate ten people at once. I guess I must give credit where credit is due, because I think he charmed the shit out of them like he does everybody. I spent most of the meeting studying this big map they had up on the wall, highlighting their claimed boundaries. They had pretty much everything marked off between 52nd and the old 205 from Mount Tabor down to Johnson Creek. What a fantasy. I wonder if the Brentwood Bernie Boys know their members of the glorious Foster-Powell Neighborhood Association. It's like they're not even living in reality.

Anyways, the committee, or whatever the hell that collective of braying jackasses they had representing them is called, agreed to work harder to keep Survivors from crossing their territory, in return for us being less aggressive in recruiting across 52nd. Of course, it was put in much nicer terms with nobody admitting any active roles either way, but I guess that's politics. I was glad to get out of there. My skin still crawls just thinking about it.

Your friend,
Leopold

July 5, 2022

Dear Friends,

It is hot as balls in this damn house. As part of the quarantine, I'm not allowed to open any of the doors or windows, so given the temperature outside of late you can probably imagine how sweltering it is inside. I've taken to wandering around in just a pair of shorts to help alleviate the problem a bit, but even then, I'm still sweating like a dirty nun come confession day. I tried taking cold baths a couple of times, but of course then I get too cold, which helps a bit when I first get out, but the overall effect doesn't last too long. About the best compromise I can figure is putting just my feet in the bath, so I've put a chair in the tub. However, of course if I sit in the bathroom all day I can't see what's happening outside. I'll be glad when this quarantine is over.

Jon Seabreeze came and talked with me a bit yesterday through the window. Oh, he talked to both me and Smiley Dave Larson when we first got back, but this time was more of a social call; checking in with me, thanking me again for my service, and asking me if there was anything I needed. I can't tell you how appreciated it was. With the exception of the person who drops food off next to the front door, who never stays to talk or anything, most people avoid getting close to the quarantine houses all together. It was nice to have someone to talk to, even for just twenty minutes. We mostly talked about the cistern project. Apparently, we've managed to get our hands on a few old above ground pools, so now they're just figuring out how best to use them.

Having Jon Seabreeze come by reminds me a lot of the first time I went into quarantine, back in the very beginning before the stay at home orders had even been issued. I'd had contact with someone most likely infected, so I stayed in my house for two weeks. It was a similar kind of deal, with a friend dropping off groceries, but otherwise pretty much everyone avoiding getting too close. Nobody said anything of course, but you could just kind of sense their unease. At least we still had the internet then, but still, human contact is human contact. Jon came and visited me a couple of times just like this time, talking to me through the window, seeing if I needed anything. He had his wife leave some cinnamon rolls by the door. I think it was then that I realized he was something truly special.

Not much else to write I'm afraid. Just hot as balls. I'm not getting my mail in here, so I have no idea how you all are doing or if Mom has finally written me. I'm very worried about her and Charlie. You never know what those Turtles might do.

Your friend,
Leopold

July 9, 2022

Dear Friends:

There must have been some crumbs out on the counter or something, because now it's covered in ants. It's almost kind of funny to think about how though so many things have changed, ants are still just as annoying as ever. I've probably squished thousands of the little buggers, but sure enough, when I come back even just an hour later there's always more of them. I guess if nothing else it gives me something to do, which is good, because I'm bored as hell.

When I'm not killing ants, I've been spending a lot of time at the front window, watching the world go by. People don't like to get too close to the quarantine houses, but there's always plenty going on within view. Right now, my personal favorite is to watch Mrs. Jacobs who lives across the street. Yesterday she was weeding the garden in front of her house, down on her hands and knees, her ample backside up in the air. I wouldn't say this in front of most people, but since we're friends, I don't mind admitting that it did something to me. I mean, she's not the loveliest woman I've ever seen, a bit heavyset and in her late forties, but it's been a while. I'll say it again, my one regret is that I bought my house in a neighborhood full of families and couples. I don't know, the last thing the Republic needs is drama. Everyone frowns on drama given we have bigger fish to fry, but still, I wonder if Mrs. Jacobs would be flattered or insulted if I told her how enticing I found her backside.

I've been having trouble sleeping of late. I've been having a lot of anxiety. I know I'm being a hypochondriac, but I keep feeling symptoms coming on, though none seem to last more than a day. I can't imagine being cooped up in this sweatbox for more than two weeks. What a nightmare that would be. I had a nightmare the other night. I was back in my house, but there were ants everywhere, pouring in via every little crack and cranny. At first, I tried to squish as many as I could, but I couldn't keep up. They were filling the house, crawling all over me. I couldn't stand it, so I smashed out a window to crawl out, but Nurse Nancy was standing in the way. She was looking at me with those tired big blue eyes, her face devoid of emotion. Her tone was similar. I know you, she said. I just stood there, unable to move as the ants completely covered my body. Good god it was horrifying. Good god I can't wait to get out of this quarantine and get back to being useful. There's nothing to do in here except sit and worry. What if I am sick? What if I have to stay here longer? What if something has happened to Mom and Charlie? What if anything? We aren't meant to be cooped up like this, but I must, for the good of those around me. This will pass, I just need to be patient.

Your friend,
Leopold

July 12, 2022

Hello Friends,

Here I am on day twelve, still showing no symptoms. Two more days to go thank god. I don't mind being honest with you, for whatever reason this time around felt harder than previous times. Maybe it's the added factor of it being hot as balls in this house? I don't know, I guess maybe it doesn't really matter given that I'm so close to the end. I keep thinking that symptoms are popping up, but of course once I quit fretting about them they fade away. When did this get so hard? I wonder how Smiley Dave Larson is doing with it. Probably just staring at the wall smiling stupidly or something. I don't think anything really phases the guy.

Throughout all of this I keep thinking back to our meeting with the Foster-Powell Neighborhood Association. They served us drinks with ice in them. Can you imagine the ostentatiousness? They must have some solar panels or a generator somewhere, maybe with a reserve of fuel to keep it going. Nearly every community does, we use ours to power a little welder when we need it, though few would waste such a limited luxury on making ice of all things. It really just goes to show you what kind of people we're dealing with. The kind who would waste one of the most precious resources just to create a false illusion for visiting dignitaries. They might as well have slapped their dicks on the table. Pathetic. Though I will admit it was amazing to have a drink that cold. I mean sure, the water out of the tap is all right, but nothing compared to this. I never thought the sound of ice clinking in a glass would make me feel emotional.

Anyways, the war with the ants continues. I've taken to squishing them with my fingers, but since they're those little sugar ants, now my hands stink like citronella. I wash them but given most of my entertainment right now is hunting down and squishing ants, there isn't much point to it other than the fact that I can't stand the smell. Mrs. Jacobs is no longer working across the street. Hopefully it wasn't because I was watching her so much. She caught me a couple of times, though I did my best not to be skeezy about it. I'll probably be forgiven, being in quarantine and all, but I'll have to watch myself better when I'm back in the real world. We're still a small community after all. The last thing I need is that kind of reputation.

Two more days. Just two more days and I'll get out of here. I miss people. I miss human interaction. I'm tired of people avoiding me. Not even the person who drops off my food will make eye contact. I'm not sick, but until I emerge, I might as well be in the eyes of my compatriots. This is the right thing to do, we must protect the Republic, but god that doesn't mean I can't hate the experience.

Leopold

July 15, 2022

Hello Friends,

I'm free. I'm free. I'm free. Thank fricking god I'm free. I remember when I got out of quarantine the first time, back when the first wave was just beginning. I went out and ran some fifteen miles until my knees gave out, then I hobbled another five. I went clear down into Oaks Bottom and then up around above it, looking out across the river and downtown. It was glorious. People were still out and about back then, though even by that time they were sticking more and more to just their neighborhoods. People were just starting to give leery looks to people they didn't recognize. It was a strange experience. The stay at home orders were issued while I was in quarantine. So, the world I emerged into was entirely different than the one I left behind. Crazy to think about. It seems like an entirely different world. More like a story I remember reading.

No time for running this time around. Things are buzzing here and everyone needs to help. The mid-summer vegetable harvest is in full swing, which of course means the canning and drying season has begun, and other projects are moving forward. We have a ton of zucchini. Remember how hard people used to always try to get rid of their zucchini because they always planted too many? I can remember people sneaking them into my car when I was at parties. Seems pretty funny now. Anyways, I'm helping bury an old hot tub to use as a cistern. We're putting it six feet down, so it doesn't freeze during the winter. We're hoping the lid with some reinforcement will handle the weight of the dirt. It's quite the hole we're digging. It's a real beast, a big 800 gallon bastard. We've got a couple of others of various sizes, so it's going to be a good start to collecting our own water in case the taps ever run dry. We're setting it up so gutters will flow into them. We've got a Boomer named Chuck Henderson who's clever about these kinds of things. He comes out and works with the rest of us. He isn't a shut-in like a lot of his generation, though I guess I can understand why most of them would be that way.

I see I have a big pile of mail from you, so I'm looking forward to going through it. Got a letter from Mom and Charlie, thank god. It sounds like a lot has been going on east of the mountains, but I'll fill you in later. Right now, I want to just go to bed. You're going to get a shit ton of letters of me. This one and everything I wrote in quarantine, minus two I burned when I wasn't doing so well mentally. Sometimes what happens in quarantine stays in quarantine.

Cheers,
Leopold

July 17, 2022

Dear Friends,

I'm so glad to have read in your letters that you are doing well, though it's crazy to me that you haven't formed up with your neighbors to create some kind of collective, if not for the mutual defense at least when growing vegetables. No household should be an island in times like these. We are stronger together than alone. I know that I keep hammering on this point, but at times I feel you are still stuck in the past, thinking always of what used to be rather than what could be. If you're going to just sit and wait longingly for a vaccine to magically appear, then what makes you any different than those who have posters of the Cheetoh hanging in their houses? I know you don't like it when I get preachy as you call it, but why wait for change when instead you can be part of the change we all need?

Take for example my letter from Mom and Charlie. It's nearly a month old, which should show you the current state of things over in the so-called safe zone. Apparently, some wheat fields in the area have been getting set on fire, on purpose, and the Turtles wrangled up some people and shot them to make an example. Mom says most were Survivors, though two of them were locals, one being a guy I went to high school with named Sam Donaldson. He ran the little newspaper in my hometown. Mom seems pretty okay with everything, but I can't imagine her ever being supportive of people lighting fields on fire. She seemed a little surprised that Sam was involved, but she said apparently his editorials had been getting more radical of late. The rest of her letter is a lot of the usual rhetoric about farmers feeding the nation, the need to keep the food supply secure, and the such.

Personally, I don't trust the Turtles much, not after what they did during the riots in those so-called camps they set up in the valley south of here. I get they had to do something, what with all the violence between the locals and the runners, but I still can't stomach what were pretty much internment camps. I mean, what the hell were they expecting to happen? Everyone panicking all to shit and they try to forcefully pack people into camps? Lunacy. I mean sure, something had to be done, but that was the best they could come up with? Nothing but a bunch of goose stepping fascists if you ask me. Wonder what's going on in the valley these days? We don't get much news from that far south. I doubt the old adage of no news is good news really works anymore. Anyways, that's probably enough yammering from me. I'll try to make my next letter more cheerful. Take care, stay safe, and tell Danny to keep his head above water, or at least as much as possible. I think he'll feel better if you start working towards something.

Your friend,
Leopold

July 24, 2022

Dear Friends,

It's been an interesting week. Somebody up in the northwest
quadrant has been flushing rags rather than burying them in one
of the pits and it clogged the sewer system for the whole area.
We're talking water coming up in at least fifteen households
every time somebody flushed or ran the tap. Not a good
situation as you can probably imagine. It caused quite a debate
about how to fix it. Chuck Henderson was convinced that we
could probably fix it on our own, but we really don't have
anybody who has done that kind of work before, so in the end
Jon Seabreeze decided we needed to swallow our pride a bit and
write a letter to the Essentials to see about getting it fixed. Some
of the more independent minded didn't agree with the decision,
but I think it was the right one. Might as well use them while we
have them.

I got to be part of the group that escorted them when they
arrived, mostly to make sure our folks kept their distance. We
had them scrub themselves down with alcohol when they
reached the boundary, but still, the less contact the better. They
came on an ATV pulling a trailer with all their equipment on it,
four of them all together, three maintenance and one cop. I had
heard rumors that some Essentials got attacked down around
Johnson Creek, so I guess it must be true if they're being
escorted now. They were of course all wearing protective suits,
which must have been hot as hell, especially once they located
where the clog was and started going at the street with pickaxes.
Jon Seabreeze was generous with them, he told us to keep our

distance so they could take off their hoods if they wanted to for a little air or water. Of course, we still stayed close enough so we could tell what they were doing, so we can do it ourselves next time. Old Chuck even got up on a roof so he could get a better view.

I was kind of shocked to see that the cop was my old neighbor. Glad to see she's still kicking. She took off her hood for a drink of water and left it off for a while to cool off a bit. She was pretty damn sweaty. I kept trying to discern any kind of emotion on her face, but she had her cop mask on pretty well, you know, stone faced. It has to be kind of weird to be back in your old stomping grounds again, but she didn't give any clues about what she might be thinking. I did catch her looking introspective with a bit of a frown on her face, but she put her hood back on soon after so didn't get to discern much else. I don't know, it's not like I ever talked to her that much when we were neighbors. It was just weird to see her again. Anyways, they arrived in the morning and got it all fixed up by the evening. We escorted them back out and that was that. I hope you're all doing well. My apologies if I got a little too ranty in my last letter. It would be good to hear from you again.

Leopold

July 27, 2022

Dear Friends,

We nearly had a bad accident today with another hot tub we're turning into a cistern. We'd gotten the hole dug and were working together getting the big old bastard into it when the ground along the edge of the hole gave way under the feet of Jennifer Higby. She slid partway into the hole before the people next to her managed to grab her and the hot tub went sliding in, pinning one of her legs, shattering her femur. The screaming was terrible. It seemed to take forever for us to lever it back off of her, though it couldn't have been more than a moment or two. The sight of her leg flopping around all loose was horrifying to look at. I had to go puke in the bushes when it was all done. Chelsea Hernandez, who used to be a veterinarian, set Jennifer's leg with a splint and gave her some aspirin. Nobody argued whether or not she really needed it. Jennifer's wife seemed pretty distraught about the whole thing. She just sat there on their couch after checking on Jennifer. Can't say that I really blame her. I'd probably be the same way. Just the thought of the sound when the bone broke still makes me sick to my stomach. God I hope she's going to be okay. Such things are bound to happen, but we all have to be much more careful than we used to be. Jon and Joanna Seabreeze came to see Jennifer, they stayed for about an hour, which given how busy both of them are, just shows how much they care for all of us. Thank god for them and this community they've built.

I got another letter from Mom, this one only a few weeks old, so I guess things must be calming down again east of the mountains. The wheat harvest sounds like it's in full swing and the yields are looking good in their area. They heard that a combine caught fire over by Wasco and burned up quite a few acres before they could get a plow around it. Mom says such things are becoming more common since it's getting harder to get parts and people are increasingly having to fix things the best they can. The Turtle administrators claim they're doing the best they can, though I doubt there's really all that much they can do. Even in the old days the combine parts that didn't come from overseas had to at least come clear from the Midwest. Hard to imagine things coming from that far, but I guess they're still getting diesel from somewhere so there must still be some trains or long-haul trucks running. Hard to imagine. Almost makes one mad to think about, how they just left us here to die. Imagine it's this way in pretty much any major city, all of us non-essentials left behind. Screw them. We're making something here. All they're doing is scrambling to hold onto the last crumbling bits of the old world.

Anyways, I better close. They don't have me working patrols anymore since I got put on the cistern project, but I still like to volunteer to help out some nights. Take care.

Leopold

July 31, 2022

Dear Friends,

Well, the bastards have finally gone and done it. The Brentwood Bernie Boys and the Warrenites over at Reed blew up into an all out riot at the Safeway drop point. The truck was maybe only halfway empty when the usual jeering turned into a couple rocks getting thrown back and forth and then without warning an all out brawl. The driver wasted no time. He got on the intercom and yelled something about no service for the next few months and the handler sprayed some bullets over everybody's heads to keep them away from the truck while they pulled away. We skedaddled back within our own boundary as quickly as we could. For the past couple days we keep hearing gunshots to the south and several buildings are on fire, so the stupid bastards must still be at it, probably both blaming the other for the truck leaving. Fricking idiots.

Of course this all started quite a panic here in the People's Republic of 47th and Long, but I think we will be okay. We've been pretty damn proactive in making sure we grow enough vegetables to go around, though I imagine a lot of us are going to get to missing flour before the truck comes back, if they do, not to mention protein. I feel pretty bad for the independent households, I don't think a lot of them have enough to go around. We'll of course welcome in anyone who wants to join the Republic, as long as they're relatively close that is. The Bernie Boys and Warrenites can starve for all I care.

There's a lot of talk around here about getting us some chickens or goats. We have a couple of the former, but only from a few old backyard hobbies, and none of the latter. It's been discussed a lot before, but I think we're going to have to do something. Jon Seabreeze always says we need to be as self-reliant as possible, and this just really proves the point. There are so many things completely out of our control that affect us, and I imagine it's only going to get worse as time goes on. We can either sit and wait placidly for life to get more difficult, or we can get off our asses and start getting ready. I know which one I'll pick every time.

I've been helping full time with patrols again of late. Gary Gunderson has doubled the number of people doing patrols. It will slow down some other projects, but it's important to be careful right now. I spent part of yesterday just sitting on a roof near the southern boundary, watching houses burning. The last thing we need is a conflagration like what used to happen. The idea of the whole neighborhood going up is scary as hell. Anyways, I better get going. Let Danny know that I thought the story about him and your neighbor was hilarious. Take care.

Your friend,
Leopold

August 3, 2022

Dear Friends:

The whole area south of Woodstock seems to be on fire, the winds are pushing it more towards Brentwood, but everyone is keeping a close eye on things in case it starts moving this way. Nobody wants to see another Oak Grove. I don't mind seeing the Bernie Boys go up, lit by their own hubris, but it's terrible for all the independent households in the area. We've had a number just south of the Republic's boundary start asking about joining. Nothing quite like chaos to get people craving community. There's been a number of wandering households as well, most likely already burnt out. A couple have asked if they could come into the Republic. We've let in a few, but overall I think everyone is a little leery of letting in too many at once. After all, we have to quarantine them and the few we've already let in have already filled all the quarantine houses we have. I've heard the Foster-Powell Neighborhood Association is letting people in willy nilly. Probably going to get an outbreak if they aren't careful, you never know when you might get a Mary. About a year ago the Lents Collective east of here let in some wanderers and got a Mary or two. Damn virus swept through them pretty well. That's the last thing we need here. We have protocols for this kind of stuff. It's one thing if they're coming in with a house where they can self-quarantine, it's another with wanderers. We only have so many quarantine houses set up. Jon Seabreeze will come up with something. We could probably use some of the empty houses along the boundary if needed, though if they're not set up to be properly cleaned, we'd probably have to burn them, which isn't ideal.

Is it getting smoky in your area? Even before the Warrenites and Bernie Boys started torching houses it's been a bit hazy here. Forest fires I imagine up in the mountains. Not so much effort to fight them these days I guess. Some pretty spectacular sunsets, but I'd much prefer less smoke in the air. I'll mark that down as another thing to put on my wish list. As they say, you can wish in one hand and crap in the other and see which gets filled up first.

There's still quite a bit of talk here about figuring out ways to get chickens and goats to boost our self-reliance. I think this time around something is actually going to happen, though I'm not sure what. Both are pretty hot commodities in this area, so we'd probably have to go aways to find anyone willing to trade. There's a lot to think about with something like this. I can't imagine anything is going to happen until things calm down a bit. We still hear gunshots on a daily basis. Hopefully things are more peaceful on your side of the Great River.

Your friend,
Leopold

August 5, 2022

Hello Friends,

I was sitting up on my roof today, watching the flames in the distance. The fires have spread right up into Brentwood now. Who knows who originally set them, probably a mix of both the Bernie Boys and the Warrenites, but it's definitely the Bernie Boys who are taking the brunt of it now. I feel terrible for all the people caught in the middle, there's a lot of independent households in Brentwood, but there's not much we can do about it now. Jon Seabreeze has some of us converting empty houses along the boundary into quarantine houses, but we don't really have much linoleum and glossy paint, so I don't know how good they'll be. Probably have to burn them or something after they get used a few times.

For some reason while I was sitting up on my roof, I thought about when I lost my job back at the tail end of the first wave. Of course, lots of us lost our jobs around then, what with the stay at home orders basically shutting down whole swaths of the economy. I can remember how upset I was by it. How unfair it all seemed and how helpless I felt. Seems kind of silly now, all the worries and all the fears about losing a job. There are always things to do, though sometimes people need pointed in the right direction to do them.

I remember back when this all got started, and we all still thought things were eventually going to go back to normal. I used to joke that our theoretical grandchildren would someday have to interview their elders about the outbreak for a class project. I thought it would be hilarious to see the looks of confusion on their faces when all any of us old farts talked about was some TV show about a bunch of crazy people and tigers. Funny how much things have shifted. It all happened so quickly. You wouldn't think it would have, but there you go. It's amazing how quickly normal became very different.

Sometimes it's weird to think back, but one thing hasn't changed. I still think that it was an inflection point in history. A moment when the world shifts and is never the same again. In many ways I think we're better off. We're building something better here in the People's Republic of 47th and Long, something that most definitely would not have happened in the old world. Oh, don't get me wrong, we have our problems and challenges, but I truly do think the end result will be better. I've never felt such a sense of purpose before. I end each day feeling satisfied with the work I do, knowing everything helps my community. What a waste it was to live so much of my life in ignorance of such things.

Cheers,
Leopold

August 8, 2022

Hello Friends,

A few members of one of the refugee families we let in are sick. From the description of the symptoms my guess is it's just a bad cold, but still, one can never be too careful. Thank goodness for quarantine protocols. Still though, having sick people about is making a lot of people nervous. Sometimes it seems like people are always looking for a reason to panic. Brentwood is still burning, though it's more of a few scattered fires rather than a conflagration. Hopefully the Bernie Boys, or whomever in the hell is in charge down there now, is playing it safe, using hoses to soak neighboring houses so it doesn't spread any further. We're all feeling very lucky, one bad shift in the wind and it could've been the Republic on fire.

In other big news, it sounds like we're definitely going to send out a group to acquire more chickens and goats for the Republic. Some of the more vegetarian minded put up a lot of resistance to the idea, but Jon Seabreeze thinks it's an important step to us becoming self-sustaining. They're putting together an expedition and Jon himself asked me to join. It's quite an honor. There's going to be twenty of us or so, all on bikes, most hauling trailers. They've put Gary Gunderson in charge, which doesn't seem like the best choice to me, but I think they're worried about encountering Survivors or god only knows what. We're going to go south to visit the King of Milwaukie, which is only four miles or so away, but anymore four miles might as well be forty. Plus, if we do get any goats or chickens, it's going to be slow coming back. I'm nervous about going, and not looking forward to another two weeks of quarantine, but still, it's quite an honor to be chosen.

I've heard rumors that there's been some kind of crazy shit going on up north of you in Mill Plain. Some crazy stories about a death cult or something? Bunch of people offing themselves to reach the promised land, you know, the usual rigmarole. Have you heard anything about that? Probably inflated by rumors, you know how it gets with a game of telephone. Essentials, especially the postal ones, love to gossip when they get the chance, or sometimes somebody on patrol will yell back and forth with somebody outside the boundary. Sounds a little nuts to me, but I guess you never know. I guess I could see something like that happening, after all, it even happened in the old days, but I can't see it being all that common. I don't know. Probably just rumors.

Anyways, hope everyone is doing well. Be sure to give Danny some shit for me.

Cheers,
Leopold

August 10, 2022

Dear Friends,

Hello from the so-called Kingdom of Milwaukie. We left
midday and got here a few hours later. We would've gotten here
quicker, but we had a small standoff with a group of twenty or so
Survivors up in the burnt out area that used to be Brentwood and
a second time with a group of ten when crossing Johnson Creek.
Both times they whooped and hollered for a while, but then
decided we weren't worth tackling. The fact that a number of us
are carrying guns probably didn't hurt anything. It was kind of
surreal biking through the still smoldering ruins of Brentwood.
There were a few little knots of former inhabitants here and
there, but not many.

The Kingdom of Milwaukie is really just a double lot down in
Linwood with a barricade around it mostly built out cars on their
sides and other such things. The King of Milwaukie is a
sometimes jovial, sometimes serious fellow with wild hair
sticking up and a walrus moustache. When we arrived, he was
in a pair of basketball shorts, jogging laps around the perimeter.
His wife, called the Prime Minister, used an infrared
thermometer on all of us before we were let inside, but otherwise
neither of them seemed that concerned. Maybe they're
Survivors or something. Not all Survivors are crazy asswipes. I
for one kept my mask on and made sure to stay six feet away
from them. I wonder how many batteries they have for that
thermometer? We didn't hoard enough early on, so the Republic
doesn't have any left. Anyways, the King has quite a reputation
as a tinkerer, so it sounds like pretty much everyone leaves him

alone since he's willing to provide his services to just about anyone in return for trade, either goods or labor. It's basically a trading post for this whole area.

The Kingdom includes a house and well equipped shop, with the rest of the interior almost entirely devoted to vegetable gardens. They even had some pot plants growing. One whole corner was fenced off, inside of which was fifty or so chickens. Once inside it became obvious that the King had no interest in what we had brought for exchange for what he wanted; vegetables, a tank of gas, some bottles of ethanol, a transplanted little apple tree, and other various things which the King politely called crap. Gary Gunderson spent about an hour talking to him, and finally found out that the King wants much the same as we do, to get his hands on some goats. If we had some goats to trade, he'd gladly give us some chickens. The King said he knows there's some goats below the Great Burn, we'd just need to go down to Gladstone and talk to Reverend Inch down at the High Rocks. So there you go, now tomorrow we're headed down to Gladstone. Looks like this is going to turn out to be a real adventure. Hopefully this letter gets to you, the Prime Minister promised to hand it off when the Essential post comes through.

Leopold

August 11, 2022

Dear Friends,

Hello from Gladstone, the furthest I've been away from the Republic in nearly two years. It's kind of funny to think about given that it's only ten miles distant, which would put it about the same I guess if I came north and visited you. To be fair, we'll never actually get to go into Gladstone. We were met by a patrol of theirs about a quarter mile distant and escorted around the perimeter to the old pedestrian bridge across the Clackamas at High Rocks. I hear it's the only bridge still standing for miles. You can see the remains of the old 205 bridge just upriver and what's left of the old 99 bridge downriver. It's no wonder that the Reverend Inch and those he affectionately calls his goons guard it so carefully. They have sandbags and folks with machine guns on either end. It appears that the Reverend and his goons live a life apart from the people of Gladstone, or at least that's the sense I got. Some type of symbiotic relationship. I'll be glad to be able to get back home.

It didn't take us long to get here. Significant parts of Milwaukie and pretty much everything south of the Expressway is completely burned out, consumed by the chaos of the second wave. It's one thing to hear about something, it's a whole other situation to actually see it. I thought Brentwood was bad, but here pretty much anything of wood has been burnt down to the ground. The only parts of Gladstone that remain are right up against the river. In some places even the asphalt was warped the fires got so hot. It was definitely a sobering experience to see it. Definitely made me feel lucky to live where I do.

It's no wonder that the Reverend and his goons all look rather hard and rough around the edges. I imagine most were in some way involved in the riots, one way or another. The Reverend himself is covered in tattoos, even on his face. Gary called him a pirate when he went through our stuff for the toll to cross the bridge, which made the Reverend laugh, but he did say we could camp nearby for the night and told us where to find a man named Munson who always has goats to trade. Gary asked him what things are like across the bridge. He just laughed, a rather off-putting sound, and said a group as big as ours should be fine if we didn't stay too long. I for one am all for that. I can remember a lot of the news stories from the valley when things were getting bad, and none of them sounded good. I have a hard time imagining things have improved that much.

Hopefully this letter will get to you. I miss home and look forward to getting back.

Your friend,
Leopold

August 13, 2022

Hello Friends,

We crossed back over the bridge at High Rocks in the late afternoon. The Reverend of course demanded another toll for crossing. We gave him a couple of goats and that seemed to please the bastard well enough. As you can probably surmise by our payment, our trip across was a success, though it took longer than expected. It wasn't hard to find this Munson character, he and his goats were on an old driving range not far from the bridge, but he proved to be a rather difficult character to negotiate with. It was strange how different it felt once we crossed the bridge. There's been a general sense of unease since we left the Republic, but it seemed to grow by ten times the moment we got south of the Clackamas. For nearly a day and a half the bastard toyed with us, making outrageous demands, even at one point insisting that we give him all of our bikes, but in the end we managed to convince him to see the greater needs of the group over the individual. I doubt he was as happy as he could be with the transaction, but I don't think any of us are that pleased with it either. No matter, because we crossed the bridge successful.

Munson was a tall swaggering man, with wild stretched out features and a penchant for bravado in manner and dress. None of us ever got closer to him than twenty feet. He was a Mary, a walking incubator, something he proudly told us the moment we found him, delighting at the sight of us backing away. I guess it makes sense. How else could a man live down here alone and remain unmolested? My skin is still crawling just thinking about being as close to him as we were. To be honest, I'm even leery of touching the goats we got from him, though of course such a phobia is ridiculous. I think he completely flustered Gary Gunderson. Every counteroffer was a fifteen minute soliloquy containing inadvertent riddles which had to be teased out. He even demanded a kiss from Leslie Hayes at one moment, which is understandable only given who wouldn't want to kiss Leslie Hayes, but it was still inappropriate. Gary of course didn't even consider such a ludicrous demand. In the end Munson seemed just glad to have someone to talk to, which I imagine goes a long ways to explaining why he dragged it out so long.

I think the Reverend was rather surprised to see us come back so successful. You could see it on his face when we first showed back up to the bridge, but he hid it well fairly quickly. He offered us the same camping spot on the north side, and of course we took him up on it. Things are going to be slower going with all of these goats. I can't wait to get home. I can't wait to be nestled again in the warm embrace of the Republic, safe from the chaos of this outer world. I've seen enough to sate my curiosity most likely for some time. No matter though, we have done our part to assure the Republic will have a long future. That's what's important.

Leopold

August 22, 2022

Hello Friends,

Did you ever watch a show called Sunday Silver Screen? It was a TV show that was on Sunday afternoons when I was a kid, I think on CBS, or maybe NBC. Anyways, it showed movies ranging from the 1940's through the 1970's, though you really never knew what you were going to get. Some days it might be a delightful family comedy or even at times a cartoon, while other times it was some B-movie slasher flick sure to give whatever impressionable minds were foolish enough to watch nightmares for at least a week. Regardless, every Sunday I took the risk, my parents too sure in their faith of the sanctity of Sunday afternoon television to ever catch on to what was going on. Sometimes life is like that.

For instance, there aren't enough quarantine houses to go around, so we've had to double up. I'm stuck with Aaron Meeker, who to be frank is a god damn chatterbox who never shuts up. I would've much preferred to have been stuck with Leslie Hayes, but of course her boyfriend for life, or whatever the hell it is people who commit for life call themselves anymore, valiantly volunteered to risk his own life to be with her through quarantine. Clever bastard, I mean sure there's a risk, but in the meantime, they get what amounts to a two week romantic vacation while I have to sit here constantly telling Aaron Meeker that I don't want to talk about the god damn trip south. We were both fricking there, so what's the point in talking about it? I guess I can at least be glad that I'm not stuck in quarantine with Gary Gunderson. The thought of being stuck in close quarters with him for two weeks makes my skin crawl. Don't get me wrong, he's effective at what he does, but he has one of those smiles that never goes past his mouth. He might as well have doll eyes. It's a little disconcerting.

Anyways, sorry I haven't bothered to write any letters until now, but I was exhausted after getting back and as you already know there's a chance that any letters I write in here will never even get to you. Aaron and I aren't even in one of the normal quarantine houses, just an abandoned house on the west edge of the Republic which they will undoubtedly burn if either one of us falls sick. We don't even really have furniture, just some old blankets to sleep on. Aaron, when he isn't trying to yammer my ear off, tends to spend a lot of time staring out the window, so I have to sit near the back of the house and stare at an old backyard of overgrown grass and rhododendrons to avoid him, which isn't exactly the most exciting thing in the world. At least Aaron gets to watch the patrols walk by. Sorry for the sweat stains on this letter. It's hot as balls in here.

Your friend,
Leopold

August 24, 2022

Hello Friends,

I can remember taking several long bike rides back when the first wave was subsiding, but we were still in lockdown mode. It was something to do, something to fill the time that didn't involve Zoom meetings or watching Netflix. One time I rode down the Springwater Corridor all the way to Boring and back. I didn't plan on doing it when I left the house, so as you can probably imagine I was pretty thirsty by the time I got done. Another time I rode my bike south to Oregon City and then back north along the west side of the Willamette to Sellwood. Actually crossed at the same pedestrian bridge at High Rocks. How very different it was then. I can remember riding through Lake Oswego. It was the first real nice summer day in May. There was a park with a beach and it was just packed, hundreds of people all crammed together, practically nobody wearing masks. It really came as no surprise to me when that area was one of the first and hardest hit in the second wave. Bunch of rich idiots, and of course they got in their cars and scattered when things got really bad. Bastards. Who knows how much they helped spread things around.

Anyways, it's kind of surreal to think how different riding down to Oregon City felt this time around. It felt so much further away. I don't know. I can remember years ago going to Ireland and visiting various relatives. I was near Dublin, staying with a third cousin, and they were giving me contact information and directions for visiting some other relative on the west side of the island. My third cousin was lamenting the fact that they hadn't seen these particular relatives in more than a decade, but they just lived so far away. It was a three hour drive. Just goes to show you how variable and relative the size of the world is I guess. It's kind of funny to think about how big the world is now. How can we ever explain such things to the children who will have no memory of it? I guess maybe that's not going to be my problem. Just funny to think about.

Jon Seabreeze came by earlier today to visit, which was quite decent of him, and Joanna Seabreeze made us some cookies which she left by the door, which is really decent considering that without the Safeway trucks we aren't getting any flour. Jon thanked us again for our help in procuring the needed goats and chickens. He told us we should be proud, which I guess I am. He didn't stay long, which is understandable, after all he is a very busy man. Lots of people are depending on him. I hope everyone north of the Great River is doing well and you're all taking care of each other. In times like these it's important that we all do whatever we can to help.

Your friend,
Leopold

August 25, 2022

Dear Friends,

Leslie Hayes is sick. Smiley Dave Larson came around and
asked everybody who went south whether or not we have any
symptoms. Apparently, she has a fever and a sore throat. Of
course, the minute Dave mentioned the symptoms, Aaron
Meeker became convinced that he had the same symptoms too. I
think it's a bunch of bullshit, given he never once complained
about having any symptoms until after Dave mentioned Leslie
was sick, people are like that, but who knows. I for one don't
feel sick, though I will admit my throat has felt scratchy since
Dave knocked on our front window. It's probably nothing to
worry about, except for the fact that we'll all probably have to
stay longer in quarantine, which is bound to drive me nuts.
Aaron is freaking the hell out, and keeps saying things like, "this
is what we get," or "I've got it, I know I've got it." On the plus
side, if he does have it, at least a sore throat might shut him up.

I'd never admit it to Aaron, but I am worried. We came into
contact with a lot of outsiders on the trip south. We know
Munson was a Mary, but what about any of the others? Let's
face it, the Reverend and his goons are most likely Survivors, so
god only knows how many Mary's might be in that rabble. We
kept our distance and wore masks of course, but there's always
mistakes and missteps. We're all human after all. Good god I
hope it can't be true. Can you imagine how things would change
if I got sick. I guess I could handle dying if it was my time, but
what if I had to leave the Republic? Even if I recovered, there
would be no way to tell whether or not I was a Mary until it was

too late. Where would I go? What would I do? I can't imagine. Even as I write this I can feel the sweat coalescing on my brow, but it's hot as hell in here, so of course I'd be sweating. I'm not worried. I'm scared. Everything I've worked for could be for nothing in an instant.

What if we're all carriers? Thank god for the quarantine protocols. Maybe if I stayed in quarantine long enough they'd let me stay, even if I did have the virus. Maybe somebody could volunteer to come in with me to prove I'm not a Mary. We've allowed it a few times before, but it was always some loved one who was willing to possibly sacrifice themselves. Who in the hell would do it for me? I'm guessing Leslie's boyfriend is feeling like a big chump right now. Look what his grand romantic gesture got him. I need to do something to distract myself. Things are going to be okay. I just have to stay positive and things are going to be okay. There's lots of reasons why people get fevers and sore throats. It doesn't mean she has the virus.

I don't know why I'm writing this letter, given you might never see it.

Leopold

August 27, 2022

Dearest Friends,

Aaron Meeker won't shut up. He just keeps blabbering on and on, convinced that we're most definitely going to die in this stripped down house and that this is what we get. I wish he would just be quiet already. Don't get me wrong, I'm most certainly worried about the same thing, but I don't see the point of hammering away at it day and night. Even if we are sick, statistically speaking we probably won't die, so at the very least he could freak out about real problems, like what the hell happens afterward if we survive. We haven't really heard much more beyond the fact that Leslie Hayes is sick, but by the sounds of it nobody else has fallen ill. You'd think if one of us were going to fall ill then all of us would fall ill. I have a hard time seeing how only one of us could have been exposed. Aaron is in one of the bedrooms crying right now because I told him to shut the hell up already. I've been spending most of my time in the kitchen, smushing ants.

Joanna Seabreeze came by yesterday with a letter from Mom and Charlie. She asked my permission to open it and then read it aloud to me through the window. I thought it was quite decent of her. I focused my entire attention on every single word, drinking it in for the mental nourishment I've been missing. She asked if I was feeling okay, and you could tell that she actually cared, that she wasn't just being polite or probing for information to alleviate the worries of the community. It's times like these that it all seems worth it. Yes, I might get sick, but I'd do it all again. Joanna and her husband have created something unique here. Something worth dying for if you ask me. Charlie and Mom both seem fine, there was little in the letter of any substance except it sounds like the wheat harvest went pretty well without major incident. It probably means Mom is mad at me still for again refusing to go be with them. She just can't seem to wrap her head around what we're creating here.

I had a dream about Nurse Nancy last night. We were all at a rave or something, dancing like mad in wildly flashing lights. She was there for some reason, but so were a lot of random people, even that crazy goat guy Munson. The dancing got a little out of control and people started bumping and jostling into each other, people started getting knocked down. She was one of them. She looked up at me, her face blank, and said, "I know you." I just kept dancing. We all kept dancing. It was a weird dream. Such things were never really my scene. I hope you all are all right. I hope that you get to read this letter.

Your friend,
Leopold

August 28, 2022

Hello Friends,

Leslie Hayes has gonorrhea, or at least that's what they think now. Smiley Dave Larson wouldn't say too many details, except that some further symptoms definitely all point to a sexually transmitted disease. Thank god. They're going to keep us in quarantine a bit longer to watch all of us, but all in all it looks like we're in the clear. Aaron Meeker is practically dancing with joy, but I'm trying to be a bit more subdued. After all, no reason to carry on like a crazy person. But still, it feels like a huge weight has been lifted from my chest.

I bet it's fairly awkward right now over in Leslie's quarantine house. Dave mentioned that there is a bit of a debate about whether or not to give her any of our limited supply of antibiotics given she kind of brought it on herself. It's not like you accidentally get gonorrhea. I wonder where she did get it? My guess is from one of the Reverend's goons down by the bridge at High Rocks. A number of them definitely seemed to have their heads on a swivel, eyeing what I imagine to them was some new blood. There was even a woman eyeing me, but of course I didn't do anything. She was a petite little thing with the sides of her head shaved. Pretty cute, but still, not worth the risk. The last thing we need is to bring something into the community like Leslie did. It's called being responsible. I'm sure there's likely already consequences being discussed. Though perhaps being locked in a hot house with the person you cheated on will be punishment enough. What could she have been thinking?

I guess perhaps I shouldn't judge so much. I don't know, if I truly had an opportunity with that woman down at High Rocks, say she came into my tent in the middle of the night, could I honestly say that I wouldn't have done something similar? I'd like to think the answer is no, but there's a part of me that knows I probably would. It's been a while since I've been with someone in such a way, and though I know what my duty is to my community, we all have an animalistic part of us that at times just cannot be denied. Perhaps it would be best for me to remember that.

Hopefully all of you are doing well and disease free. I'm looking forward to sending most of these letters to you, I'm likely only going to burn one this time, and seeing what letters you have sent me. I can't tell you how important this link to another part of the world has been to me. I think we're building a better world here in the Republic, but I miss the wider world we once inhabited. I must forget it now though. We cannot go back, we can only go forward.

Cheers,
Leopold

September 3, 2022

Dear Friends,

I still have my old iPhone. Is it strange that I still have it? Sometimes I get it out and hold it in my hand. Sometimes I run my finger along the screen as though I'm scrolling down the information superhighway. I don't know. There's something comforting about it. Back when it still had some battery power left in it, I used to turn it on about once a month, just to see if maybe it wouldn't still connect to some tower that got missed or something, but of course it never did. Just the same old no service message over and over again until finally the battery gave out and that was it. I think that was the moment I truly fully understood that I had to start looking forward. There was going to be no going back.

Even now it's strange to think back at how insane things became during the second wave, how crazy people went as they realized how this time around was going to be worse. People didn't want to believe it, others became so scared they couldn't think straight. I did as I was told. I stayed in my home and watched the world go mad. It all went so quickly. I don't think anybody understood how rapidly chaos could become the norm. Then the towers began to come down, then the electrical lines, and then the world was so very much smaller, while at the same time suddenly bigger. What would things have been like if somebody like Jon Seabreeze hadn't been around? Somebody who didn't panic. Somebody who created a sense of order when nobody else could. We started with so little, yet here we are, building something more than we had before. I'm a lucky man, no matter what else, I know I'm a lucky man.

Jon Seabreeze came around and thanked every one of us as we came out of quarantine, even Leslie Hayes whom it was decided would get the needed antibiotics. They had a big picnic for us amongst the trees of old Woodstock Park, the part we left in grass as a common area. Janet Hicks, who runs the stills, allowed some of her alcohol to be watered down so the twenty of us who went south could have proper drinks like in the old days. I was hungover the whole next day. Jon Seabreeze himself led a toast in our honor. I can't tell you how good it felt to see all those glasses held high.

I read through all of your letters. I'm glad you are all doing fine. It sounded like quite a scare with that group of Survivors moving through the area. I'm glad to hear you and your neighbors are forming a local watch to ensure something like that doesn't happen again. This is a time for us to be together. This is a time for something beyond ourselves. This is a time for community.

Your friend,
Leopold

September 10, 2022

Hello Friends,

I spent most of today up in a tree, or rather several trees to be more specific. We're cutting branches off to use as firewood for this winter. Not too many of course, we want the trees to grow back and prosper, but enough where we won't freeze if the wood trucks don't start coming next month. We really have no reason to think they won't come, but of course the Safeway trucks haven't come since the Warrenites and Bernie Boys got into it, and nobody really seems all that sure whether or not they're ever coming back. I guess in some ways it's been a bit of a boon. Lots of independents on all sides have suddenly found a new interest in the benefits of a collective community. We've added so many households in the past month that there's talk on whether or not we need to slow down adding new ones, you know, to ensure our supplies for the winter. I don't think it will be a problem, but you know how people get. Smiley Dave Larson especially has been getting himself all worked up, but he seems more concerned with the fact that a number of these new households are from east of 52nd. He thinks the dolts at the Foster-Powell Neighborhood Association won't take kindly to this.

Despite these little quibbles, things all together seem quieter here now than they were a month ago, which I'm glad to see. For a bit there things seemed a bit too much like the bad old days for my preference. Those on patrol haven't even reported a single sighting of any Survivors for the past two weeks. Personally, I'm looking forward to staying close to home. Spending time in quarantine twice during a single summer was a little much for me. Don't get me wrong, it was part of my duty, but still, I don't think it's wrong to have a preference.

I greatly enjoyed your last letter. It sounds like you have quite a few characters in your area, though I'm glad that everyone seems able to put aside their differences enough to work towards the common good. Who knows, maybe before you know it you'll be writing me letters telling me to get my ass up there because of how good you have it. The early days of organizing are always the most exciting. That sense of hope returning. I wish the letters I got from Mom could contain even half the good news as the ones you send me. It sounds like the Turtles are really cracking down on the other side of the mountains, and all Mom can do is talk about the good old days. It's pretty depressing. She keeps going on about vaccines, and even brings up the Cheetoh every now and again, which is something she never did when he was still alive. Anyways, tell Danny congratulations from me for getting elected Block Captain. It's quite an honor. Maybe he'll be the next Jon Seabreeze.

Cheers,
Leopold

September 16, 2022

Hello Friends,

Janet Hicks, who runs the stills, was kind enough to give me a little extra for personal use if you know what I mean, so please excuse the scrawl. Of course, all the alcohol she makes is supposed to be used for disinfection purposes, but Janet is a good egg who recognizes that sometimes people need a little extra something every now and again. It's not a bad thing to cut loose, you know, as long as it doesn't become a habit. We've all seen some shit after all. We can't pretend that it isn't true. We can't just sit around and play pretend.

God damn do I ever miss toilet paper. Wiping our asses with rags, and how long can that fricking last until we're all out of rags, even if we clean them, which is a whole other level of gross I never thought would be a normal in my life. What then? Will everyone just go back to the right hand left hand rule? Nobody ever talks about this kind of shit. I had a little stash hidden away, only a couple of rolls, but I managed to make them last for months, doing just one square at a time. I can't tell you how depressed I was when the last of them got used up. Washing fucking rags in the god damn sink. It's disgusting. What's the point of worrying about it I guess, it's not going to change anything. We want a better world, fine, but the cost is wiping your ass with a god damn rag.

Nearly hurt myself today, or rather some other idiot nearly hurt me. We were cutting branches out of trees. Some idiot overhead let a big old bastard drop without warning and if I had been just a foot or two over it would have landed right on top of me. Scared the crap out of me though. You should have heard the tirade I unleashed on him. I know, you might think I went a bit overboard, but damn it, do you know what can happen if somebody gets hurt? This isn't like the old days. We've got to be more careful. We don't have room for stupid mishaps.

I had a dream last night. I was down across the bridge at High Rocks again, out on that driving range surrounded by goats. Munson was there, blathering on and on about wanting someone to give him a kiss for a goat. He just wouldn't shut up, wouldn't see reason. I lost my temper and punched him in his face. I just kept punching and punching and punching. Good god what a nightmare. I woke up in a cold sweat and couldn't get back to sleep again. I don't know, maybe that's why I yelled so much at the poor sap up in the tree. But still, we can't be having stupid easily preventable accidents. We don't live in the old world anymore, and it's about time people get it through their god damn skulls.

Your Friend,
Leopold

September 20, 2022

Hello Friends,

Was it wrong to beat up the jogger? I'm helping store
vegetables in roots cellars today. We dug out a lot of root cellars
last year. Jon Seabreeze has us keep track of everything closely.
As an accredited accountant, he is a real numbers man, which
makes sense with things like this. We need to keep track of what
we have to make sure we'll have enough. Numbers are
important. Everything needs to be accounted for. To be honest,
I spent a good part of the day worried that people could smell my
breath. Janet is a good egg. So perhaps I let my mind wander a
bit to distract myself from such worries. Maybe that's why I
thought about the jogger.

It seems like a strange question to pose to oneself now. After all,
it was several years ago, back when the second wave was just
ramping up and we were starting to come to grips with what was
happening, though of course it took some longer than others.
This guy had the habit of running through the neighborhood. He
didn't live in the neighborhood or anything, he just ran through
it, probably on his way to the trails at Reed College or
something. I don't know. All we knew was that he was a man
with a habit. Oh, he didn't show up every day, just every now
and again. You remember how quickly people started to get
sick, how people panicked and pushed back when the second
stay at home order was issued. People were scared. We needed
leadership, and Jon Seabreeze stepped up, getting everyone to
agree to cordon off the neighborhood. It wasn't that hard, most
people inside and out were doing their best to avoid each other.

Not the jogger though. He didn't seem to have a care in the world, and he didn't seem to give a shit beyond anyone but himself. When we decided to close off our little area, we told him to please run around, he ignored us. The next time he did it we yelled at him to stop. He yelled back that we had no right to tell him what to do. He tried to run down the street. We tried to stop him. I can't remember who threw the first punch, but we made short work of him. We didn't do any permanent damage, we just wanted him to stop running through. The Republic was small back then, it wasn't even the Republic yet, it would've been easy for him to run around, but he just refused to do it, yammering on about his rights. He was pretty banged up by the time we were done with him, though again, nothing permanent, though we did break his nose so perhaps it never quite looked the same. I don't know. We never saw the guy again, so we must have scared him enough to get it through his head. I think it was the right thing to do. Everything we have now, everything that we have built better, is because it was the right thing to do. None of us wanted to beat up the jogger, but he refused to give us any other choice.

Your friend,
Leopold

September 25, 2022

Hello Friends,

The leaves are beginning to turn, and it rained today. I was glad to get your letter. It sounds like you and your neighbors have a really good thing going up there. I'm glad to report that a Safeway truck showed up here a few days ago. I was supposed to go help bring back our share but was asked to stay and help pick some apples. It's a pretty good sized tree, so there were quite a few. I'm glad for the change. I don't feel like going outside the boundary. My hands have been shaking of late and I've been having a bit of trouble focusing, so doing something automatic seemed like the better idea. Smiley Dave Lawson picked for a bit too. He was talking a lot like he always does, but I wasn't really listening. Something about the Foster-Powell Neighborhood Association again. Probably pissed about the houses east of 52nd joining the Republic. That usually seems to be their big complaint. Assholes.

Sometimes I feel like a fraud. I've been here a long time. So many other of the originals have carved out niches for themselves, but not me. Sometimes I just feel like I'm floating along, not truly doing my part. The Republic has given me so much. What have I truly given it? I could do so much more if I'd just believe in myself a bit. It was this way in the old world too. All those splits in the road, I always took the path of least resistance. Now here I am, just as unimportant as I've always been. I know it can't be entirely true. There's been so many times Jon Seabreeze himself has thanked me for the work I've done. He and others seem to believe in me. I just wish I could do the same for myself.

I felt a little shaky after picking apples for a few hours, so I went home to lie down. I didn't really feel sick, just shaky, that's all. Definitely not sick. Mrs. Jacobs was in her yard, digging out potatoes. I laid down in my old easy chair next to the window so I could watch her work. I kept my eyes partially closed so she'd think I was asleep. I watched her backside up in the air while she went up one row, and then catch glimpses down her shirt as she went down the next. There's something enticing about her, though I'm not sure what it is. Maybe it's because she's right in front of me. Maybe because a fantasy is better than nothing at all. I imagined her noticing me watching her. I imagined her looking up and smiling at me enticingly. The kind of smile that tells you she's flattered by your attention, that she welcomes it. I didn't imagine anything else. There wasn't really a need. I already had what I truly wanted. God how I miss that look from another, that sizzle between two people. God I miss so many things.

Your friend,
Leopold

September 29, 2022

Hello Friends,

We're going to have to get Danny a dress uniform with all the responsibility he's been given, maybe something with epaulets or something. Just kidding of course. I can't say how proud I am. I didn't know he had it in him. Of course, I imagine he's getting a lot of help from somebody in the background who doesn't like the limelight, though perhaps I'm just speculating. I wouldn't worry about it too much. People tend to know where the real power lies in these things. Though to be honest, it feels kind of strange that it tends to be that way.

Oh, don't think I haven't noticed the strange predilection towards masculine leadership that still seems to pervade our world. I know it's not like this everywhere. For instance, I know the leadership of the Warrenites down at Reed and the Foster-Powell Neighborhood Association tend to be majority feminine, and though I never met her, I've heard the leader of Gladstone is a woman as well, though that whole situation is strange with the Reverend Inch and his goons protecting Gladstone, but not really living in Gladstone. I don't know, I'd like to write it off as just coincidence, but that doesn't seem right. Is there just some biological need for somebody thumping their chest in the midst of chaos, or are we still carrying more of the scars of the old world then we are willing to admit? It's strange to think about, given that so much of how we live our lives here in the Republic is based on creating a world free of the wrongs of the past. Maybe we just need to wait for the next generation, those who don't remember the old world and who have only been immersed in new ideas, but aren't they influenced by how things are now? I wish I could talk to Joanna Seabreeze about it. I'm sure she'd have some interesting thoughts on the subject. Janet Hicks has some opinions, but most of hers seem to revolve around the idea that men are animals good for little beyond breeding. I'm not sure she's the best person to ask.

I don't know. I was thinking the other day about my last job before I got laid off. The guy was a real dumb ass who was too proud and stupid to ever admit that he had no idea what he was doing. He had this sycophant who he kept lavishing with praise and responsibilities even though the guy never did his work and lied about it all the time. Basically the people who got laid off were the ones who kept bringing up the problems in the department. It's stupid, but thinking about it still makes me mad. It doesn't make any sense. It has absolutely zero relevance in the world today, but I'm still mad about it. We're such funny creatures.

Your friend,
Leopold

October 3, 2022

Dear Friends,

It's raining here today, so I imagine it is raining there as well.
It's been raining the past few days as I'm sure you're fully
aware, though perhaps it's not been raining there. The weather
has always been funny here. I worked for a bit in the rain,
helping cut branches, but then felt a chill going on so went inside
to rest. Now it's dumping buckets and everyone else has gone
inside as well, so I guess it's no big deal. There is not much to
write about. It's been gloomy here and I feel much the same.

Today I was thinking about the riots. It seems strange since they
weren't really all that long ago, but I can't really seem to
remember if the second wave started first or if they started
first. Probably not all that important. Like most things, it
doesn't really matter which one started first, because they
certainly helped each other along once they got started. I don't
know, looking back, some of the riots seem right while others
seem wrong. The protests seemed better, when they were
peaceful. I don't know. It all seems so long ago. I went to a
couple of the protests, back in the early days, in the strange lull
when people had calmed down enough to stop rioting and we
hadn't figured out how fast the second wave was spreading. I
can remember so many different feelings. Fear, but with a good
mixture of hope that maybe we could truly build something
better. That maybe we could actually fix some of the last ills of
our ancestors. Then of course everything went to shit and so
many things got forgotten, both good and bad. It's always
amazed me how long people continued protesting and rioting,

even as it became obvious that the second time around would be so much worse than the first. People rioting, people fleeing, whole neighborhoods on fire, the whole system collapsing in on itself. Jon Seabreeze made us a refuge, a peaceful island in a stormy sea. I felt hope again when the Republic came along. A sense again that despite all the fear, here was an opportunity to do better. It's strange to think that in the old world I never even talked to my neighbors beyond a hello.

When we came back north the King of Milwaukie wouldn't let us back inside his compound, or I guess technically his Prime Minister a.k.a. wife wouldn't let us in. They at least traded us goats for chickens as they earlier agreed, even a rooster which is hard to find, though it seemed like she didn't even want to do that. I don't know. People are strange. They get weird ideas. It must be nice to change one's mind on a whim. I don't know. I'm rambling a lot here. I better close. Give Danny a salute for me.

Your friend,
Leopold

October 7, 2022

Hello Friends,

I'm lonely. There, I said it out loud, though I imagine you have probably guessed it. Perhaps I've always been lonely, it's just that before I could pretend that things would someday be different, back before the world shrank to just a few square miles. Maybe it's being here that is doing me in. Maybe if I left and explored the world again, pretended that things were like they once were. I don't know. I believe in what we are doing here, I believe in it so much, but I am lonely, and I can't pretend that it's not true. I don't want to be alone. I don't want to feel isolated, but I do. I've worked hard to help make things as they are, but there is nothing for me beyond my own needs. There's nothing concrete driving me, simply a sense that it is the right thing to do. Perhaps fulfillment requires the completion of the biological drive, the sense that you have some skin in the game. I don't know, and I'm guessing I never will.

Sometimes on the rare occasions when the Safeway truck brings condoms there's always a scuffle to claim them. A chance to break away from the time tables of the rhythm method or the risks of pulling out. A taste of the freedom we once enjoyed before we squandered it away with all of our other luxuries. One more thing lost to the hubris of the old world. I used to fight for my fair share, even though I had no need, because I used to hope that perhaps things would be different. I haven't bothered in more than a year. What's the point? Someone might as well get the enjoyment. They do no good in my dresser drawer. I don't even know if the Safeway trucks still bring them. People don't talk about that kind of stuff as much as they used to, at least not here. Somehow it has become dirty again, nobody's business though rumors spread fast in small communities. I remember back in the old world, once there was this underground mining town in Australia where there were ten men for every woman. The mayor got in trouble for making some comment about how it was the perfect place for an unattractive woman to move, because even a three would become a ten. There was all sorts of an uproar about it, with people demanding he apologize, but he wouldn't, because it was true. God, I remember when the first lock down began, and everyone was talking to each on Zoom and Facebook. People got crazy, clothes came off, it was as if the world was ending and inhibitions no longer had a place in their lives. God what a heady time. Then it all became normal, and people quit doing such things, or perhaps it was just me.

I need to quit bitching. To build a better world Jon Seabreeze says there must be sacrifices. Perhaps this is just my sacrifice. It probably isn't much of a price to pay, or at least that's what I like to keep telling myself.

Leopold

October 9, 2022

Dear Friends,

It's still fricking raining out. It's been raining for days on end it seems with no sign that it's going to let up any time soon. It's starting to drive me crazy. I can't seem to get warm. All I do is shiver even though I'm packed under blankets. Maybe my blood is getting too thin. Maybe I'm just going a little nuts. I don't know. Thank god for Janet Hicks right now. She's my savior. I'm having dreams again, every night this week I've had one. The one last night was especially disturbing. People were yelling at me, telling me what to do, but I didn't want to do whatever it was they wanted me to do. The whole crowd was literally seething, spit flying out of their mouths they were so angry. I was having a panic attack. I kept spinning around looking for someone, anyone who wasn't yelling. That's when I saw her, Nurse Nancy, looking at me with that emotionless face. Just staring at me. It was horrible.

Do you remember that time down at the Goodfoot, when we went to hear the funk band? It was back when Danny was still dating Nancy. You remember, the night he saw the girl he'd been dating right before Nancy, the one he still had a hard on for? What was her name? Rami, I think, that sounds right. Anyways, they went outside together and Nancy got upset. You were dancing with some guy you'd just met and so I had to sit there so she'd have someone to talk with. She was upset, not like crying upset. She just kept going and going, and I just sat there in my drunken stupor, and all I could think was how much I wanted to kiss her right then. What would have happened if I had tried to kiss her right then? Would she have kissed me back, or would she have slapped me? I guess I'll never know. I never got a chance to ask. She broke up with Danny right after that of course. Danny was with Rami again for maybe a week before she was gone again too. All of it just seems so crazy now.

I've heard the patrols around the boundary are starting to see small groups of Survivors again. Not many, just little groups here and there wandering in the rain. They don't seem to be causing any trouble, none of the usual chest thumping or anything like that, but it still makes me uncomfortable. What if the Foster-Powell Neighborhood Association is letting them through again? What then? God it's too much to think about. I'm tired. It's late. This candle is starting to burn down low. I better blow it out before I pass out. I hope you're all doing well. I miss you all so very much.

Your dear friend,
Leopold

October 15, 2022

Hello Friends,

The first wood truck arrived yesterday. A big beast full of rounds which we packed back to the Republic and set to splitting with mauls with a vigor. My head hurt with every swing, but it was almost a good kind of hurt, like a lover scratching your back in a fit of passion. They used to send us the wood already pre-cut, but I guess at some point they figured it would just be easier to send us a bunch of mauls and splitting wedges and let us go to it ourselves. Eventually I imagine they'll just give us saws and roll whole logs off for us. I imagine too some winter soon they'll just quit coming. I'm not sure what we'll do then. How many more years do we have? How many more years until the Turtles tighten their grip too hard and the last vestiges of the rotted out frame collapses. Who knows, can't be too many more years I imagine. I just hope we're ready for when it does.

I can remember the first day I really felt hope again after everything went to shit. Not the little twinges one forces themselves to have just to get by in their day to day. No, I'm talking about the real sense that things are going to be okay. You know, where there's still going to be struggles, the road is uphill, but it's going somewhere. It was in the early days of the Republic, on a ferociously cold and rainy day, the kind that soaks you right through. The first wood trucks came to ensure nobody would freeze. They dumped huge piles of split wood and we went out, the whole community at the time, to help carry it back to the Republic and stack it. People were laughing and joking. Some people sang as they worked. For the first time all the things Jon Seabreeze kept telling us suddenly came together. Here we all were, working towards a single goal. The work got done so fast none of us could really believe it. Suddenly we knew that it was truly possible. We really could create a better world. Hope came alive in me again that day, something I hadn't realized was gone until I felt it again.

Have you all felt that feeling up north of the Great River yet? Has that spark caught hold and began to burn brighter? Can you feel its warmth radiating upwards through your middle? If not, I promise it will come. There will be a day when suddenly you realize that you may just be a cog in a machine, but it's a machine where every part is as needed as the next, and all of them need each other. Wonderful things are coming my friends. Wonderful things indeed.

Yours truly,
Leopold

October 17, 2022

Hello Friends,

There's been quite the hullabaloo around here of late. Ha, hullabaloo, that's a fun word to use. Anyways, they removed Janet Hicks from running the stills. Seems like she had been giving too much away for uses other than disinfectant, and most likely utilizing more than her fair share for personal uses as well. Her apprentice, Jessica Tran, has been put in charge. She's pretty straight laced, so I imagine there's going to be a lot of self-medicating people that are going to get cut off. If I'm even being honest, that list would include myself of late. It's probably for the best. I haven't been at my best over the past month or so, and I think the imbibing has definitely played a big part of it. However, there's a lot of people who must need a little help more than me, because there's a lot of people upset by the whole turn of events. Smiley Dave Larson has been walking around telling people that utilizing alcohol for drinking rather than its intended use as a disinfectant is stealing from the Republic. The little fink, I know for a fact that he's imbibed himself from time to time. I'm not sure what's going to happen to old Janet now. I'm sure they'll find something for her to do, but I can't imagine she's going to be happy with it.

In other news, we keep seeing Survivor groups pop up along the boundary, not just at night, but during the day time as well. There's talk about sending a new delegation to the Foster-Powell Neighborhood Association to discuss the problem again, but I don't know how well that will go. It sounds like they're pretty cranky with us for expanding more past 52nd. However, we weren't actively recruiting, most of those households came to us when the whole Warrenite versus Bernie Boys kerfuffle took place. Is it our fault that we offer a better option while those Foster-Powell bastards just claim households regardless of what those households want? It's a ridiculous way to run things, and given how crappily they do run things, it's only a matter of time before more households flop over to us. People are already debating about whether or not we should let that happen, especially right before winter when things get tight.

I heard from Mom the other day, the first letter I've gotten from her in a while. The Turtles shot a few more people that they're calling dissidents. Mom wasn't really sure what they did, but she's sure they must have deserved it. She doesn't really go on any more about me going to live with them. Maybe she's figured out finally that I'm better off where I am. There are apparently rumors circulating about a possible vaccine for the virus. But of course, as you know, rumors circulate all the time. If every rumor was true, we'd already have a thousand different vaccines. I think Jon Seabreeze has it right. The only hope we have is what we make ourselves.

Cheers,
Leopold

October 21, 2022

Hello Friends:

Another wood truck showed up, so I spent most of today helping split wood again. I'll be a regular Adonis by the time all is said and done, nothing but rippling muscles that glint in the sunshine. LOL. In truth I'm sore as shit and unsure if I can even lift my arms above my head, let alone go back to splitting wood again tomorrow. I guess I should be glad for the work. It felt good to sweat a little. It's amazing how a little bit of exercise can change one's whole perspective about the world. I imagine the fact that it stopped raining and we got a nice fall day probably has something to do with it as well.

Jessica Tran invited me to eat dinner with her and her husband Donovan last night. He's not really her husband, but they have been together so long they might as well be married, so I call him her husband since nobody has bothered to come up with a better name for such a situation. Jessica is a pretty good egg for somebody so straight laced. She enjoys a raunchy joke apparently. I was quite surprised at the several she told and she seemed to enjoy the ones I shot back at her. We had a pretty good time. Donovan is a quiet fellow, but fairly good at deadpan zingers. He is one of the permanent teachers at the school, focusing mostly on math. He seems like a fairly good guy, though I guess I think they make a bit of an odd pair. However, I guess that can be said for many couples. It was nice of them to invite me to eat with them. When Janet Hicks was still running the stills Jessica was always around, but I never really noticed her. However, she seems to have me pretty figured out. I went down to the stills the other day to try and see about getting a little on the side for personal uses. She invited me to dinner instead. A pretty clever way to shift the conversation if you ask me.

I'm not sure if I have much more to add. Things are getting along here well enough, with just the usual worries mentioned in earlier letters. I haven't heard from you in a bit, but I imagine perhaps things are slower than they used to be. I wonder if the Essentials are managing quite as well as they used to. It's hard to tell what is going on with the wider world, but it feels as if parts are beginning to decay. Perhaps it's just me, but it certainly feels as though it takes longer for letters to get anywhere these days. Take care of yourselves. I can't wait to hear more about what is happening up there.

Yours Truly,
Leopold

October 27, 2022

Dear Friends,

I greatly enjoyed your letter from a few days ago describing all that has been going on your side of the Great River. It really sounds like you have something good going on, and the fact that other people want to be a part of it should be more than enough proof that you're on the right track. I know it can be a little frightening at times, but we are communal animals, and we tend to do better in groups rather than alone. I can understand some of your concerns. When people suddenly realize anything is possible, they can get all sorts of crazy ideas, often wanting to throw out tried and true methods that work with all the crap that doesn't. However, I think in the long-term level heads usually prevail. You should have heard all the crazy ideas that came up when we first established the Republic. Most of us were just as scared then as you are now that things would spiral out of control. None of us wanted to end up with something similar to what happened to the Capitol Hill Autonomous Zone up in Seattle or the Old Town Democratic Cooperative here in Portland. So many things start out well, but can end badly. However, none of us wanted to stick with the mistakes of the past either, such as those morons in the Foster-Powell Neighborhood Association. In the end, I think all the difference was having somebody with a steady hand and a calm voice taking the lead. Somebody who never yelled rhetoric and always seemed to want to listen. Somebody respected by everyone, allowing them to bridge the gaps and cut through the bullshit. That was who Jon Seabreeze was for us. Perhaps you and Danny can be the ones for yours.

On that subject, I really think you should come up with some kind of a name. It seems stupid, but you would be suprised how much symbols can rally people together. Of course in choosing such things, one must be careful not to get bogged down in semantics and other pointless crap. It's better just to prod things along to happen naturally. It was Joanna Seabreeze who came up with the name People's Republic of 47th and Long, at first almost as a joke, but then it just stuck because it described so well what we were all about. She was also the one who designed our flag, basing it on the big Japanese maple in her yard.

Danny's account of the Survivor attack was quite exciting, though of course I imagine it was for frightening at the time. I'm glad to hear that you're not taking any shit from them anymore. They have no right to demand anything from anybody. What right do they have to take what everyone else works for? Screw them. Screw them all.

Yours Truly,
Leopold

November 1, 2022

Hello Friends,

Jessica Tran invited me to a get together last night at her house. She and her paperless spouse were hosting a small Halloween party. It was almost strange given how nobody really does things like that anymore, at least here. I was a bit uncomfortable with the whole thing, but it made me rather nostalgic as well. She insisted that anyone who came wear a costume, so I had to scrounge some stuff together. In the end I just wore a polo and pair of dockers I still have and went as me from the old days. Let's just say that mine was far from the most creative costume. Jessica had this whole sexy witch costume she must have saved. It looked pretty good. Her paperless spouse Donovan had calculator buttons drawn on his chest with a marker. He went to bed rather early. I knew that some people still do such things, though we really don't do scheduled official holidays anymore. When we first got things going it seemed like something from the old world worth giving up, you know, forcing one culture down the throat of another. Though of course nothing was ever done to dissuade people from celebrating their own holidays. Anyways, I stayed pretty late. I enjoyed it a lot.

Life has become a bit of a blur here over the past couple days, as being hustle to make full preparations for the coming winter. Hopefully it's a rather mild one like last year. Jon Seabreeze announced the other day that we would not be accepting any new households into the Republic until next spring. I think this is mostly to guarantee we don't strain our supplies, but also to alleviate some of the strain with the Foster-Powell

Neighborhood Association, who have been rather riled up again of late. Some people, such as Gary Gunderson, weren't all that happy with this decision. Given the Safeway trucks are still coming, they see no reason to let worries about food supplies limit our growth. However, Jon Seabreeze said it's best to get into habits before you have to. Personally, I can see it both ways, but don't really have that much of an opinion about it. I'm sure in the end, if some of the independents need our help or want to join, Jon Seabreeze will probably acquiesce. After all, though he's logical as all get out, he also has a good heart.

I heard from Mom the other day. Sounds like her and Charlie are as fine as ever. They're mostly puttering around, and Charlie is convinced we're going to get a bad winter this year because his knee is aching more than usual. Frankly I don't see how getting kicked by a horse when you were young gives you any kind of magical meteorological powers, so I don't put much weight in his prediction. Charlie has always been a bit of a character.

Cheers,
Leopold

November 3, 2022

Dear Friends,

Can you remember the last time you started dancing just out of pure joy with the world? Before I would tell you that it seemed like a lifetime ago, but Halloween night I danced like we used to when the world seemed so calm and still, and the biggest worries were nothing, but illusions crafted by our own inability to see the artificial reality around us. People beat on chairs and beatboxed, and someone even sang a song that made absolutely no sense because they were just making it up as they went. Somebody ran back to their house and got a guitar, and even Donovan got out of bed and stood in the doorway and watched us all gyrate. I twirled Jessica Tran around her living room and people laughed and hooted with delight as I dipped her nearly to the ground, her hands tightening so hard around my arms that I woke the next morning with fingertip bruises. For just a moment I felt alive again, more alive than I have in a long time. Just sheer unbridled joy without any of the tiniest of doubts or fears. What I would give to feel that way forever.

I woke up very early this morning and climbed up on my roof to watch the sunrise. The Boomers who are still afraid to mingle woke with the dawn and wandered the streets as Jon Seabreeze has declared is their right. I watched an older smiling woman brush her hands along the dried out corn stalks, her face pointed towards the sky, breath steaming into the air, enraptured by the feeling of the outside upon her. A goat who must have escaped its pen ambled by and she beamed with joy, and I found myself smiling too, proud that I had a part in this thing which made her so happy. Oh those poor Boomers who still feel afraid even here in the safety of the Republic. Shut away inside waiting for the brief hour that is theirs and theirs alone. What must it be like for them? To hide away from everything? Don't they get lonely? Don't they feel a yearning to throw their fear away regardless of the risk? Do they ever dance, or would they even try if given a chance?

I should probably quit writing and go to bed. They're increasing the number of patrols and I'm getting put back on helping walk the boundary tomorrow. They had to sound the air horns last night. Small groups of Survivors were probing the boundary. Flitting from one block to the next, on one side and then another, even via the Foster-Powell Neighborhood Association. They do nothing to stop them. Their boundary is as porous as their ideas. Things always seem to get worse in the winter. People get more desperate when it's cold.

Your friend,
Leopold

November 7, 2022

Hello Friends,

Despite all the hullabaloo mentioned in my last letter, there has been so sign of any Survivors since we put more people out on patrol. It's like they just up and completely vanished. I don't know, it makes me worry, and I'm guessing it's doing the same to Gary Gunderson because he still has all of us patrolling day and night. Maybe it's some kind of trick, you know, just trying to lull us into a false sense of calm, or maybe they've just moved on. Survivors never tend to stay anywhere for too long. Personally I wish I could go back to regular work. This walking around the boundary is getting tiresome, especially with all of various portions jutting out. There are no really significant straight lines anymore. Hell, pretty much the whole east side of the walk is on the other side of 52nd. It would be nice to be put back on general duty. Jessica Tran was showing me how the stills work. Who knows, maybe I could be the new assistant. She's rather pleasant to be around, and it would be nice to have a more permanent job.

Two people fell sick yesterday, neither people I know all that well. They probably just have colds, but they got put into the quarantine houses all the same. Better safe than sorry. There's always a few this time of year, but not as many as you there used to be back when we intermingled all willy nilly in the old days. I saw Jon Seabreeze sitting by the front window of one of the quarantine houses and talking to the woman inside. Maybe I should take the time to go talk to them too. I don't really know them that well though, so I think it would probably feel a little weird. I don't know. I probably won't. Some of us are just that kind of person, and some of us aren't. That's just the way it is. It probably explains why I'm still single.

I had a weird dream last night. We were down across the bridge at High Rocks trying to get goats out of that Munson fella. He kept saying that he'd give us some goats for a kiss, and for some reason Gary Gunderson was telling me I needed to do it. Obviously, I didn't want to. It's for the Republic he kept saying. Do it for the Republic. We need those goats. Just do it. He kept pushing more and more, and I knew he was right, but I still didn't want to do it, and then I just broke, and did it. That's when I woke up. Couldn't fall asleep for the rest of the night. It was such a weird damn dream. That's all, just a weird damn dream.

Tell Danny I expect to hear that he has some grand falutin title soon like El Presidente. Hopefully things are still going well up there and you're getting all the kinks ironed out. There's always some smoothing you have to do with these things.

Your friend,
Leopold

November 13, 2022

Hello Friends,

I'm not sure if I should tell you this, but I feel as though I should tell somebody. It's wrong. So very wrong, but yet if I'm being honest, I've never felt as alive as I did in the moment which I'm not sure I should describe. I don't know. We have been friends for a long time, so perhaps you can find it in you to not judge me too harshly for the weaknesses which we all battle from time to time. If not, I guess at the very least you are far away, though I will most definitely miss writing to you and receiving your letters, two things that have helped me keep my sanity in the worst of times. Besides, who is to say what is wrong and what is right in this new world. Who are we to judge based upon the rules of a place that only exists in memory? I've written this letter half a dozen times and ripped it to shreds nearly as many, but I feel as though I have to tell somebody. My hands are literally shaking with the memory.

I slept with Jessica Tran. I'm not sure how it happened, but it's been building over the past few weeks. At the Halloween party she seemed to grip me more tightly than needed as we danced, I thought she was just frightened of me dropping her in the dips, but no, there was more. Yesterday evening she was showing me how the stills work, our hands accidentally brushed and for a moment we both paused, seemingly luxuriating in the moment before pulling away and avoiding immediate eye contact. She invited me over for dinner. Donovan ate with us, and then sat up with us talking, but eventually grew tired and went to bed. Jessica and I stayed up late into the night, talking and joking. I don't know how it happened, we seemed to be leaning in closer together, two binary stars inevitably pulled in by each other's gravity. Our lips met. We started kissing. Good god the feeling of electricity erupting through our bodies. I could feel static flickering from my fingertips. She was on top of me. The feel of her, the smell of her, I can feel it all around me right now. She broke away. She seemed flustered. She asked if I needed anything. I told her a drink of water. She walked into the kitchen and I followed. She began to fill the glass and I pushed myself tightly against her. I could feel the heat rising off of her. I'm sorry for all of the details, but I need somebody to understand. I'm not sure exactly at what moment everything broke loose. By the time I fully realized it we had already begun and neither of us seemed to have any interest in stopping. It's not a big house. The man basically her husband was sleeping in a bedroom not that far away. It was wrong, but oh my god how right it felt. What were we thinking? What have we done? I know it was wrong, but I want so desperately to do it again.

Leopold

November 16, 2022

Hello Friends,

I know it's far too soon to hear back from you yet, but I'll admit that I'm fretting what your reaction may be to my last letter. It's so easy to judge people in situations which we do not find ourselves in, and I hope that as friends for so long even if you do not understand actions, you can at least try to see where I'm coming from. Maybe it was a mistake to send that letter to you, but I'm all twisted up inside with far too many emotions, and I don't know what else to do with them but share. Maybe this is our version of Facebook now, writing letters back and forth to a few trusted friends, though I doubt I would've put any of this on Facebook, and back then I certainly could not have seen myself in such a situation. I know I'm rambling, for which I apologize, but paper is too precious of a resource to throw this away and start again. Nothing like a limited resource to force a bit of stark honesty.

Jessica won't talk to me. She won't even look at me. When I finally wrangled myself into a position to talk to her alone, all she said was that it was a mistake and that she doesn't want to talk about it. I guess I can't blame her. I should've seen this coming. What did I expect? That she would declare her unending love for me and leave Donovan that day? This isn't a trash romance novel. I wish she would at least talk to me about it though. There are so many threads just hanging loose. I know why I did it, but why did she do it? I feel hurt, taken advantage of, while at the same time I wonder if I took advantage of her in some way too? Do I even have the right to know her why?

111

I'll admit that I'm scared. Things like this are frowned on heavily here. They aren't illegal or anything like that, but we're all stuck here together in a difficult situation with no escape, things seen as selfishly endangering what tranquility we are able to gain are heavily looked down upon by the community. Most people here are still shunning Leslie Hayes for her transgression during the goat expedition. I'm sure that in the end things settle out, people forget, because they have to, but the process is an arduous one, a probation period where you must be careful not to slip up again. Is that it? Is it not me at all, but rather a fear of what can happen if we're discovered? Damn it, I wish she would talk to me. The worst part is not the situation, but rather the complete lack of understanding what exactly the situation is. I wish you were actually here, so I had someone to talk to about it in person, but then I guess if you were here I'd probably be more afraid to talk about it to you.

Sincerely,
Leopold

November 26, 2022

Dear Friends,

I still haven't heard anything back from you. I know the
Essentials are still carrying the mail that far because Chuck
Henderson has a cousin on that side of the Great River, and he
was talking about getting a letter from him just a few days ago. I
know what I did was wrong, but please try to understand. It has
been so long since I've truly had anyone in my life in that
capacity. I know it doesn't excuse what Jessica and I did, but
please don't shun me now. I'll be honest, there have been tough
periods over the past few years, and I don't know if I would've
been able to stick them through without you. I live in a good
place, full of wonderful people, but even before things went bad
I was always an outsider, the neighbor that never talked to
people. Perhaps I could've made a greater effort, but everyone
seemed to be so much more at other stages in their lives. What
could I even have talked to them about, and why would I even
bother when all I needed to do was hop in the car and drive
fifteen minutes to see people I wanted to see? I bought this
house specifically because it was in a family neighborhood,
because that's the way I saw my future at the time, but then I
was just the bachelor living in a family neighborhood. In many
ways I'm an outsider here. So many others knew each other well
from before. I didn't really know anybody. This is a good
place, and I want to help it thrive, but sometimes I just don't feel
like it's where I belong.

This isn't a new feeling. To be honest, I've always felt this way
in most situations. Out of place, an immigrant who has gone

native, but can never truly ever fully conform. Everything seems strange and out of place, and no matter how much I resign myself to this world, I always find myself waiting expectantly for a spaceship to drop out of the sky, declaring to me that it's time to go home. Do other people feel this way? Surely many must feel this way. How could I be the only one? It doesn't make any sense to be the only one.

Do you remember that time we were at your house, back when you had that old hot tub, and we all got drunk and naked and we sat in it all night and stared up at the stars and told stories and laughed. Do you remember how I talked about how scared I was to be alone and you promised me that I would never be alone because you would always be my friend? Do you remember? Please don't forget. Please please don't forget. I need you to not forget. I need you. I've done wrong, but we've all done wrong at one time in our lives. This is the world where we must all learn to forgive.

Your friend,
Leopold

November 29, 2022

Dear Friends,

Please disregard my last letter. Your letter arrived this
morning. I could've kissed the Essential who brought it, but he
was a rough looking son of a bitch so I did not. So many
Essentials are looking haggard anymore, as though they are
aging at twice the rate of the rest of us. I don't know. They
probably are. Some things are only a matter of time.

I was horrified to read that some group of Survivors had your
house surrounded. Thank god you and your neighbors had
already organized a bit, and thank god everyone was able to
make it to your house to hold them off, though I'm sorry to hear
that a few of your neighbors' houses were burnt to the ground.
It's terrifying to think of Survivors doing something like that, but
of course they're more than capable. They don't even need a
reason, they just like to cause destruction and misery whenever
they can. They did more than their fair share, if you ask me, in
creating the world around us. They can all rot in hell for all I
care. I'm glad to hear that everyone is all right, with only a few
minor injuries. I know you said you were lucky, but I will say
that it's more than luck, it's organization and leadership. I think
the silver lining to this incident is yet to come. You are not
alone anymore, and now you know it.

Thank you for the quick note regarding my situation here. You
thinking of me given all that has happened to you makes me
proud to call you my friend. It helped me a lot. I'm glad to
know that you understand, even if what I did was wrong. As you

say, I must strive to do better, so that is what I will do. I don't think it will be possible to strive to be any worse. Jessica Tran is still not even looking at me. I guess I can understand. What am I, but a walking reminder of her own transgression. There is nothing I can offer to her right now but a memory she most likely wants to forget. I wish I could forget it, but if I'm being honest, the thought of it fills me with a deep hunger that I have not felt in a long time. I'm a starving man given a cracker, and then told there are no more crackers left. I've remembered what life tastes like, and now I am hungrier than ever.

Anyways, thank you for the invitation to come north and join you and Danny. I may consider it, though my heart is still here, in this place that I've helped to build. We've come such a long way, but there is still so much more work to do. I've done too much to build it to turn my back on it now. Take care both of you.

Your friend,
Leopold

December 6, 2022

Hello Friends,

We have about six people sick and in quarantine right now, and anyone who had contact with them has been ordered to stay in their houses. It's probably just a cold or something, but no reason to risk the possibility of something worse. It's got everybody on edge. There was even talk that maybe it's the Essentials bringing things in, though I'd be surprised given all the cleaning protocols in place. I hope they don't cut off the Essentials. I'd hate to think of what life would be without your letters. I don't think overall there is much to worry about. Jon Seabreeze has a pretty steady head on his shoulders. He bases things on logic, not emotion. Still though, even colds don't just magically appear.

I'm working night patrols again. I volunteered. It seemed like a good way to avoid the whole Jessica Tran issue. If I'm sleeping most of the day, then there's little chance of the two of us seeing each other, which is likely for the best. I don't want her to feel shitty, and certainly don't want to feel shitty either. As you've said, we're all human. Mistakes are made, and the best we can do is learn from them and move forward. I imagine it will get easier over time. Night patrols have been rather boring. Gary Gunderson keeps telling us that there's been a lot more Survivor spottings along the boundary, and that we need to stay vigilant because those Foster-Powell bastards are obviously letting them through, but I have yet to see any. Most I've seen has been a couple possums, which of course make my skin crawl, but nothing more. The other night I heard a lot of baying and saw a big group of about twenty dogs running down the street a few blocks away. There were dogs of all sizes, running together. Haven't seen any of the feral packs in quite a while. Thought they'd all been dealt with or had headed out into the countryside. I've heard that some people still have domestics, but not many. I was a little worried the pack might come this way, but they were heading towards downtown.

Got a letter from Mom, though most of two whole paragraphs was blacked out, so I guess the Turtles are censoring mail now out of the Safe Zone. Fascist bastards. Doesn't make a bit of sense, but I guess when you crave power nothing has to make sense. Nothing much to report except Charlie is sick, so Mom is going into quarantine with him and will be out of contact for a while. Not sure why she thinks it matters, I only hear from them at most once a month anymore anyways. I guess that's just the way Moms are. Probably just a cold like here, Charlie always tended to bounce back pretty quick from such things. Anyways, take care.

Yours Truly,
Leopold

December 10, 2022

Hello Friends,

I'm not sure if I'm that big of a fan of the name you all have chosen for your endeavor, though I guess it's not my place to judge. It's just that the Burnt Bridge Collective doesn't really seem to have the right connotations, but perhaps I'm just getting nit-picky. To be honest, I'm kind of just surprised that you took my advice to actually have a name. Neither one of you seemed all that interested when I suggested it. Who knows, maybe by your next letter you'll be telling me that you chose a symbol as well. Just don't choose a Japanese maple, that one is already taken thank you very much.

Not much to report here I'm glad to say. Three more people have fallen ill and got put into quarantine, but it's looking more and more like it's just a cold. At least that's the guess given nobody has developed a fever or anything like that. The night patrols remain rather quiet, despite Gary Gunderson's insistence to the contrary, with no sign of Survivors as far as I can tell. Though I did hear that pack of dogs again and saw the biggest raccoon I've ever seen a few nights ago. I've also heard that what's left of the Brentwood Bernie Boys got into a bit of a dustup with the Reed Warrenites down near the old Lewis Elementary School, but it didn't sound like much beyond a bit of chest beating. I doubt the Bernie Boys are much of a going concern since the fire took out most of Brentwood last August.

Speaking of fire, I had a weird dream about a horse on fire the other night. A bunch of houses south of the Republic were burning and this horse trotted across the boundary with its tail and mane just completely ablaze. A bunch of us ran down to scare it off because we were nervous it would set some of our houses on fire, but the damn thing wouldn't listen to us. It just kept standing there, staring blankly at us as we waved our arms and yelled at it to go away. Somebody threw a rock at it and that's when I woke up.

On the brighter side of things, I was out wandering around a bit the other morning and saw Jessica Tran walking down the cross street across the intersection about half a block away. She actually looked at me this time, though not for long, but I'm going to take it as a good sign that maybe things can get back to normal. I miss the sense of being part of something from when I was being invited o her and Donovan's get togethers, though that will probably not happen again any time soon. I also miss other things, which most definitely won't happen again, but I digress. Anyways, I better close, got to start my patrol soon.

Your friend,
Leopold

December 20, 2022

Dear Friends,

Leslie Hayes, the woman who got gonorrhea down at High Bridge, committed suicide last night. They found her body hanging from a tree in the common area that used to be Creston Park. Nobody knows how long she was out there, but they say her face was so purple it was nearly black. I have no idea how we missed her while out on patrol, given the park is part of the northern boundary along Powell, but she was down in a bowl and in the shadows. Nobody noticed her until things began to get light. This is the eleventh suicide that we've had since the inception of the Republic, though it's been a while. It's rather strange to think about. I helped dig a hole in which to bury her in the burying place, in the same park between the old swimming pool and old tennis court. Luckily, she was already wrapped in a sheet, so I didn't have to look at her. The guy helping me dig, a fellow named Jaden Johnson, decided to take a peek, but soon after said he wished he hadn't.

There was a nice funeral. Most people in the Republic showed up and there was plenty of crying and the usual funeral sorrows. Jon Seabreeze gave a nice speech about how sad it was to have the life force of one with still so much life and ability to help others quenched too early. There was a nice bit about how now we were returning her to nature, so she can nurture the earth which nurtures us. It was quite comforting to know that even in death one helps their compatriots. Quite a few other people spoke too, even her ex-boyfriend whom she gave the clap, all extolling on her virtues and what a wonderful and needed member of the community she was. Even old Gary Gunderson spoke in his gravelly nasal, promising her spirit will continue to wander the boundaries of the Republic, helping guard us from those who wish to take away everything we've built. Personally, if I die, I'd rather not continue working patrol endlessly.

At the end everyone filed past the hole, putting in a handful of dirt. After everyone was gone, Jaden and I buried her the rest of the way. She won't have a gravestone. Nobody does. We can't waste the space and it's not our way. Jon Seabreeze says we must always keep our focus to the living. It was all very strange. Throughout I tried to dig up some kind of emotion, but I just couldn't seem to do it. I just felt numb through the whole thing from start to finish. I guess it's not like I really knew Leslie that well. I could count on one hand the number of times we talked for more than a minute or two over the past year, but so many other people seemed filled with grief. I don't know. I think I'll stop here.

Your friend,
Leopold

December 24, 2022

Hello Friends,

Happy Holidays, I guess if you're still doing such things. Official holidays here caused all sorts of debate, so we basically did away with anything official, though of course everyone is still free to celebrate whatever they want however they want, within reason of course. Being a bachelor, I really have no use for holidays, and I'd say this is closer to the overall growing consensus in the Republic. Don't get me wrong, sometimes we do celebrate momentous occasions, but these normally have something to do with some achievement in the Republic itself rather than the personal beliefs of any one group of people. Overall things seem to work better this way, though we did have a bit of a problem with some of the younger people making up all sorts of personal holidays to avoid work, at least until Jon Seabreeze nipped it in the bud.

Anyways, we had a bit of snow here yesterday, just a skiff, though there's still little patches of white here and there. It's been cold, but not cold enough to start burning wood for warmth yet, resulting in most of us keeping ourselves pretty bundled up. As you can imagine, there's a lot more people than normal volunteering for cooking duties. Most people expect that we'll probably start burning next week. The communal warming houses have already been decided, and wood stacked and put at the ready. We just had another wood truck last week, though the driver said things were a bit slick in the Gorge. This of course started the usual nattering and worry about what will happen if the Safeway or wood trucks can't get through.

I imagine once the warming houses start up there will be the usual sitting around in the evening, trading stories and the such. I'm really not looking forward to it. You can of course only go to the warming house to which you are assigned, and apparently my neighbors are the most introverted and least interesting people in the Republic. Good god what I wouldn't give to have Danny here. My winter will be in dire need of a real character. Most of my evenings will likely involve playing cribbage with Mr. Jacobs, who insists on claiming points in my hand that I miss when counting. He also has an annoying habit of stating, "now this is an interesting hand," which though undeniably true, gets tiresome rather quickly. I hear some of the other warming houses elect event coordinators, somebody who knows how to get people involved, but no such luck for mine.

I'll close here. I've got to write a letter to Mom and Charlie before it gets too dark. Haven't heard anything from them. In case you were wondering, all of the people we had sick here just had colds, just as I suspected.

Leopold

December 30, 2022

Hello Friends,

They say death comes in threes, and of late I'd have to agree. You already know about Leslie Hayes a little over a week and a half ago. Unfortunately, it appears that her decision to end things got some other people thinking along the same lines. Three days ago, an older Boomer named Bert Blankenship did the same thing, pretty much in the exact same spot. I didn't really know Bert that well. He was in his sixties and one of the more shut-in Boomers, only coming out of his house in the early morning. We've still got about thirty to forty Boomers who have gone full shut-in, and quite a few more who come out, but tend to isolate themselves and keep their distance from others. I can't imagine what something like that must be like, never having any real contact at all, at this point for years. It must not have been easy for old Bert considering how he punched his own ticket. Hopefully it doesn't give anyone else any ideas. Bert's funeral was quite a bit smaller, I only went because I helped dig the grave, and Jon Seabreeze's speech was a bit more harsh than the last one, a lot more on how once you're dead that's it, no more. I think he's nervous that more people will off themselves. Not good for morale going into winter.

The third one was a kid who died today, which is particularly sad. Nobody is sure entirely what was wrong with him. It might have been appendicitis, or maybe he ingested something. The medical team here is mostly former paramedics, which are pretty good for a lot of things, but not so much with stuff like this. It happens from time to time, but it's always a tragedy when it does. I've been asked to help dig this grave as well, though I think after this I'm going to ask to not dig anymore for a while. Starts to weigh on you a bit you know. I feel strangely numb about the whole thing. Everyone else seems pretty upset. I don't know, maybe something is wrong with me. I know it's very upsetting, and when I think about it's obviously a bad thing, but I just don't feel upset about it.

It did get me to thinking about Nurse Nancy again, and all the other nurses and doctors, and all the rest of the Essentials. I still don't think we did the wrong thing making them leave, but it would be nice to have them now. What were we supposed to do though? They saw themselves as having a duty, and that trumped everything for them, even the safety and wellbeing of their neighbors. We were far from the only neighborhood to do it. During the second round they were getting sick left and right, and the last thing we needed was for them to drag the virus home with them from the charnel houses that used to be hospitals. When you're in constant contact, it's just a matter of time, no matter what kind of precautions you take. It was all just a matter of time.

Your friend,
Leopold

January 3, 2023

Dear Friends,

Happy New Year, albeit a bit late. Seems crazy to think we are now living in the world of 2023, though I guess no more strange than it seemed this time last year when we started living in the world of 2022. In this case I'm glad to get into 2023. The end of 2022 was getting pretty bleak, and I think having the sense of a new beginning, even an arbitrary one, will help morale around here. It's been pretty low of late as I mentioned in my last letter.

We got quite the New Year's surprise in that it snowed here about eight inches, which is pretty impressive for around here as you know. I imagine you have something similar, though you never know. People have been rather jolly about the whole thing. People have been sledding on the streets that slope down onto 39th and there's a ridiculous number of snow people of varying quality just about everywhere you look. Personally, I'm less of a fan, but that's probably because I'm having to plod around through it half the damn night on patrol. I've asked for a different job, maybe tending to the chickens or goats, but who knows, lots of people want to tend the chickens and goats this time of year. I will say it is peaceful at night, all the harsh angles softened by a layer of snow, plus it does get me out of having to play cribbage with Mr. Jacobs. There are always silver linings if you know where to look for them.

The Warrenites down at Reed must be having a good time with all the snow as well. In the evening you can see a big column of smoke from a bonfire and you can hear instruments and singing in the distance. Hell, they even lit off fireworks the other evening. Not sure where they got them, but they were lighting them off. I've always heard that Reed had a small nuclear reactor. I wonder what ever happened to it, or if it's still on. Be nice to have some electricity like the old days. It's probably turned off, if it still works at all. Can't imagine it would be that safe to screw around with. I once went on a date with the gal in charge of it, or used to be in charge of it I guess. She had a degree in biology, so I guess it must not have been that dangerous to be running the thing. Either way, I know it wasn't very big.

Been having my Nurse Nancy dream again, the one where she's just looking at me all dead faced, saying I know you. Probably because of thinking about what happened to that kid who died. Do you remember when we used to go down to The Lutz all the time? Was that where Danny originally met her? I can't remember, it all seems so long ago anymore.

Cheers,
Leopold

January 6, 2023

Hello Friends,

Well, it snowed again, so we have about a foot built up here now, which is the most snow I've seen in a while. I'm sure if we still had any news to watch there would be all sorts of headlines about Snowocalypse or Snowmageddon or whatever the hell stupid name they decided to use. Anyways, it's got some people worked a bit up because there are worries that the Safeway and wood trucks might not be able to get through. I'm not too worried, we have a lot of canned vegetables and the such. Situations like this are the whole reason we're striving for self-sufficiency. I swear, sometimes it's like people aren't even paying attention. Besides, when in the hell has snow ever lasted more than a week here?

Do you remember that year we had that really bad snow this time of year, and the three of us were going to that concert at the Crystal Ballroom downtown, but the band never showed up because their bus got stuck on I5? Remember, we were sitting in the bar drinking, watching cars skid down the hill and making bets on what ones wouldn't be able to stop in time at the intersection. The whole thing was hilarious until that one car hit the side of the bus. Don't know why that memory popped in my head. I think we went out driving afterwards because there were hardly any cars on the road and we could do fish tails around the corners. Strange to think about.

Things have been a bit strange around here now as well. We've started seeing a lot more Survivors wandering around again, especially on the east boundary, which means those Foster-Powell bastards most definitely aren't doing anything about them. I imagine the winter gets a bit difficult if you're a Survivor, but that gives them no right to try and take what we've worked so hard to build. Bastards don't know anything but how to destroy. If they're cold now, maybe they should have thought about it before they started tearing down the cell towers and power lines. Stupid bastards.

Anyways, I hope you're doing all right up there. Maybe Danny can make you some snow angels like he did that one time. He was so drunk they all looked like they were disabled in one way or another. You're probably going to get a whole bunch of letters at once. The Essential carrying the mail has been a bit slower than normal, which makes sense given all this snow. I'm surprised they keep doing it all. What in the hell keeps driving them to do it? I don't know, Essentials are funny people. They've got all sorts of high minded ideas in their heads. Imagine it won't last forever. Eventually we'll have to learn to fully stand on our own two feet.

Your friend,
Leopold

January 10, 2023

Dear Friends,

I was thinking about Charlie today, back when I was a kid and he used to take me fishing even though neither one of us ever had a fishing license. He'd always tell me not to tell the kids at school. We used to climb down into this canyon with rimrocks all around the edge, down to this creek at the bottom which he always claimed was his secret fishing spot. Looking back, I'm pretty sure we were trespassing, which was really just Charlie's personality to a T. He's always been an odd duck, but I guess he made a pretty good stepdad all things considered, and he definitely made Mom happy. It would be good to hear from them soon. I'll admit that I do worry about them living over there in the Safe Zone with those fascist Turtles. God only knows what kind of crazy things can happen with those kinds of asshats in charge. Censoring letters is never a good sign that things are going well. I remember what the bastards did down in the camps in the countryside around here during the second wave. Yes, things most definitely got out of hand, especially with all the people streaming out of the cities and fighting with the locals, then the fires, but there was no reason to start rounding up people and putting them into what were basically concentration camps. Of course, people started getting sick faster, what in the hell else did they think was going to happen? At the very least I guess a lot of those fucking Turtles got sick too. A lot of them deserved it if you ask me.

I don't know, maybe I'm being a little harsh. Things got crazy when the second wave peaked. Not all of us were lucky enough to have a Jon Seabreeze around to keep people calm and collected. Lots of people did stupid things, which just resulted in other people doing stupid things, so on and so forth until the whole world was nothing but a whole collection of stupid. I remember how scared I was back then. I'm sure you were as well. God only knows what kind of stupid shit I might have done if I hadn't been lucky enough to be living here. The end of the world was a messy deal. There's never going to be any clear cut answers about it, though I still think it doesn't excuse those who acted the worse.

I can't remember why I originally started writing this letter. There was something I wanted to say, but now I can't remember what it was and I'm about out of paper. I guess it will come back to me if it's important. I can't imagine you minding another letter. The snow is starting to melt pretty rapidly here. The snow people are beginning to look pretty beleaguered. Take care.

Your friend,
Leopold

January 16, 2023

Hello Friends,

We had to sound the air horns last night. Several groups of Survivors were probing the boundary and it got to the point that we could no longer be sure that a group of them might not have gotten around us. It caused quite a panic as you can probably imagine. Everyone is pretty fed up with the situation, especially since the Foster-Powell Neighborhood Association seems to have zero interest in upholding their end of any agreements we have with them concerning not allowing these Survivor groups to tramp around all willy nilly. Personally, I fully agree with this sentiment. Jon Seabreeze has decided to send another delegation into Foster-Powell, similar to the one we did last year. Smiley Dave Larson will be leading it again of course. He asked me to come again, but I declined. Twice in quarantine last year was enough for me for a while.

There are rumors circulating that quite a number of people have died of the virus down in Milwaukie. I've heard that it's bad enough that not even the Essentials are going down there anymore. No idea if it's true, but it was an Essential mail carrier that I heard it from, so I'd assume he probably knows. If it's true, it sounds like maybe the biggest outbreak around here since the second wave. From everything I've heard, and saw during the trip to High Rocks, a lot of people down there aren't as careful as we are, so I could see it spreading pretty quickly there if it started popping up. We haven't had a case here in over a year, and our protective measures are a big reason for it. I'm telling you, with your Burnt River Collective, be sure to stake a boundary and keep out outsiders. You never know when things might get bad again. People forget so easily how quickly things can go to shit.

The whole thing is only adding to people's nervousness around here. There was even talk of barring mail from coming in, though luckily Jon Seabreeze put an end to such talk, though we aren't going to be allowing any Essentials in any time soon. If you want to mail a letter, now you have to give it to Gary Gunderson and he delivers them all to the carrier at the boundary. He also takes the incoming mail and holds onto it for a couple of days to give any germs a further chance to die. This seems a little ridiculous to me given all the safety protocols already going on, but it makes people feel better, so I guess I'm just going to have to live with it.

Pretty much all the snow is melted now, except for the remains of some of the larger snow people. I guess it was exciting while it lasted. Hope you're both doing well. Tell Danny his drawing is getting better.

Cheers,
Leopold

January 18, 2023

Hello Friends,

The meeting with the Foster-Powell Neighborhood Association did not go well. I could tell almost immediately when Smiley Dave Larson returned not so smiley. Jessica Tran's boy toy, Donovan, didn't look so happy either. Smiley Dave took him to the meeting when I decided not to go. Apparently, the Foster-Powell Council of Elders, or whatever the hell name they decided to give themselves, were a much bigger group of jackasses than normal. Smiley Dave told me all about it when I went to the quarantine house to visit him through the window. I figured Jon Seabreeze always does it, so I should probably be doing it as well. Either way, Smiley Dave told me the Foster-Powell folks basically denied that Survivors were even crossing their territory, calling it a fabrication of ours to create excuses to expand further. Even Smiley Dave had a hard time keeping things diplomatic after that, and it only got worse from there when they started blathering on and on about a vaccine surely coming soon. Smiley Dave seemed pretty frustrated, but even more he seemed dejected that he had let everyone down. Donovan seems rather more chipper about the whole thing. Yes, I went and saw him as well. He wasn't happy about the meeting but seemed rather pleased that he'd have a lot of extra time for reading.

I must admit that I'm feeling almost manic with energy of late, probably because I don't have enough to do. When I'm out on patrol I keep having to slow myself down to ensure I don't catch up with the person patrolling in front of me. Everyone is a bit wound up with high expectations that a Survivor attack is likely just around the corner, and I've never done well with doing nothing, but I think it's more than that. I don't know, I guess part of it is I feel useful again. I keep finding myself things to do to help, which makes me feel good about myself, so I keep looking for more things to do to help. Just yesterday I helped put a tarp on a leaking roof, and the day before I refereed a soccer game in the rain for some of the kids. I've even played a couple of games of cribbage with Mr. Jacobs, which seems to please him even though he's still annoying as hell.

Despite recent fears to the contrary, a Safeway truck came two days ago, and a wood truck is expected to arrive next week, though we have plenty of wood thanks to the strict rationing we have implemented. Things are good down here in the Republic of 47th and Long. I wish the same to you and your Collective of Burning Creek.

Cheers,
Leopold

January 23, 2023

Hello Friends,

I don't know whether to be elated, ashamed, or some devilish combination of the two. It has happened again, repeatedly, and I'm a mess of emotions, fears, and unbridled joy. I've slept with Jessica Tran, multiple times over the past few days. I'm not sure what happened. She was no longer overtly avoiding me, but neither were we having much contact with each other. An unspoken truce to contain our shame at the events of last fall. She needed somebody to help her with the stills. Jon Seabreeze asked me to do it because I had helped with the stills before. How could he know? How could either of us refuse without questions being pondered? We both did what we had to do. There wasn't much conversation beyond simple instructions and acknowledgement of the instructions. There wasn't even much eye contact between the two of us. But then I needed to help her drag a heavy vat out of a corner. We were in close proximity. I was overwhelmed by the smell of her. It seemed as though some great hand came out of the sky and suddenly pushed us together. I don't know what happened. One moment we were dragging the vat, then we were all over each other, down on the cold concrete floor, going at it like wild animals. I was no longer a man and she was no longer a woman, we were conduits for some greater cosmic energy.

It's an insatiable energy. We did it again that evening, right before I had to go out on patrol. I snuck behind her house and knocked on the backdoor. She opened it and let me in. We didn't even say a word. We just started again, first in the kitchen, then in the living room, then on the bed she shares with Donovan. Poor stupid quarantined Donovan. Does he know? Does he know the energy that flows between this woman and myself? I came again in the morning when my patrol was done, then again in the middle of the day amongst the stills. I've lost count. It's as though we've both gone completely mad. How can it be that nobody has noticed? How long can it be until we get caught?

Part of me doesn't care. People are growing more nervous. Voices have a frantic edge. The virus is definitely down in Milwaukie, spreading from household to household. Rumor has it that even the King of Milwaukie himself is sick. People are becoming more and more anxious about Survivors, though we see them less and less at night. Gary Gunderson and many of those like him are becoming more openly hostile in their statements about Foster-Powell. There is an edge to everything. You can feel the collective energy of so many people crammed together and increasingly unsure, and in the middle of all of it, Jessica and I increasingly cutting off the outside world with its rules and responsibilities. Freeing ourselves to take our true forms.

Leopold

January 30, 2023

Hello Friends,

I hope you can forgive me as easily as you did before, though I must admit that even if you cannot I don't think I can stop myself. The unwritten rules of our community mean nothing to me now. There is only the enrapturing cocoon of our passions. We are both gripped by a madness completely out of our control. I'm scared of myself in some ways, but my blood roars in my ears in a way I never thought possible. I even snuck away from a patrol one night. Honestly, it's the only thing about what has been happening which causes me to feel any shame. I am no longer fully human. Rational thought has taken a back seat. I know that I am gleefully running towards my ruin. I have no idea how we have not been caught, for we are doing a ridiculously shit job of hiding our activities. I think the only saving grace is that people are so caught up in the growing chaos of the outside world that they are having difficulty seeing what's right in front of their faces.

I'm no fool. I know it can't go on. Donovan gets out of quarantine in two days. Jessica Tran and I don't speak of it, indeed if I'm being honest, we speak very little if at all, but I can see the growing disconnect in her eyes. She's preparing herself for the moment we both know is coming. In a rational world we would stop, weaning ourselves of this need, but neither of us have such willpower. No, this will be a sharp cut, going cold turkey as they used to say. We are both preparing for the violent jolt of the stop. If anything, it has driven us to new heights of depravity, snapping every chain holding us back, knowing that we will both soon be tied back down to the expectations of our world once again.

We're not as free as we thought we were. We no longer have the anonymity of the masses and the safety of our numbers. No, we are all in smaller ponds now, and all the rules have changed because of it. I do not want to say such times were better. No, life in the Republic is preferable to the old alternatives, but we have sacrificed something in the name of safety and order. We have lifted it onto the table and cut out its still beating heart, lifting it high into the air for the cheering masses to see.

I must be careful. I'm most certainly manic, which means what follows is likely to be equally as dark. The higher one flies the further they fall. I must be careful. I don't want to be careful. I want to live with wild abandon while I can, for it won't be long until the sacrifice must be made again. I want to say these things to her. I want to express beyond the physical. I dare not. We are being selfish. There are things of great importance outside of us. This cannot go on.

Leopold

February 2, 2023

Hello Friends,

She's gone. Completely disappeared. Donovan and Smiley Dave Larson got out of quarantine, and Donovan went home to find her gone. He didn't tell anybody until that evening, thinking perhaps she was just out and about, but she's gone, and that is all there is to it. Where in the hell would she even go? It doesn't make any sense to me. We all know that there are other places out there, communities like ours, but how many would accept in an outsider? Especially now with what's going on down in Milwaukie. I can't imagine those places that would accept somebody in a time like this would last long. Even the dumb asses over in the Foster-Powell Neighborhood Association are cognitive of that. What is she going to do? Wander around like some kind of modern day ronin? How long can that last until some group of Survivors finds you and has their way with you? None of it makes a damn bit of sense.

Why would she do it? Things aren't perfect here of course, but we are still a hell of a lot better off than so many other places. I can't imagine anyone thinking otherwise. She never gave any sign that she was thinking about something like this. There was no warning or preponderance of evidence. Though to be fair, I guess we rarely talked about much of anything not directly related to what we were doing. I hope we don't find her the way we found Leslie Hayes. I don't think Jessica would do something like that, and we searched the Republic just in case, but I never thought she would just disappear one day either.

They asked old Janet Hicks if she wanted her job back working with the stills, but she just laughed at them and told them to fuck off. She's always been eccentric, but anymore she's getting downright nutty. This leaves Jessica's apprentice, a younger guy named Kaden Ortiz, and myself, who has a little knowledge from last fall, to try and combine our know-how enough to keep the stills going. The Republic needs its disinfectant. Kaden is a nice enough guy, but sometimes when we look at each other, or talk about Jessica leaving, I wonder if I was the only one. Was I special, or just another option, a means to an end? I wonder if Donovan knows what was going on. If he does, he's giving no sign. He seems upset, but not as upset as I would imagine. They probably actually talked to each other, so maybe for him there were more signs.

Why did she leave? Why didn't she ask me to go with her?

Leopold

February 11, 2023

Hello Friends,

Not much to report I guess, but here I am writing anyways. Still fairly despondent about the whole Jessica Tran thing. None of it makes much sense at all, though perhaps that's just the way it has to be. I remember Charlie once telling me that not everything in the world is meant to make sense, and I've been telling myself that over and over again. It seems to help, at least somewhat. I wonder if any of it really even makes sense to Jessica? We're funny creatures. So much of what we do is based on impulse so often. The old fight or flight mechanism kicking in, overwhelming logic with the need to do something. I guess I'll never know where Jessica was on the spectrum when she left. Just another one of those things I'm not meant to know. I wonder where she is right now? Does she still think she made the right choice, or did she think she made so many bad choices that something had to be done? I wish I could talk to her.

Donovan seems pretty beat up about the whole thing. I guess for him it must be even more of a mystery than it is for me. Can you live with someone for years and just be caught completely by surprise? Can you be so utterly and completely unaware despite being in such close contact day in and day out? Apparently you can, because he seems to be at a complete loss, which probably provides some clues why she acted the way she did in the first place. There is no relationship, romantic or otherwise, where someone wants to feel like they're just part of the scenery. I don't know, maybe I'm being unfair. Maybe Jessica played her cards so tight that it was impossible to see any problems boiling under the surface. It wouldn't be the first time in this world. Most of us suck so badly at communication.

I've thought about going and visiting Donovan, maybe telling him about the advice that Charlie gave me. It might help him, but it feels like a weird thing to do. I played my part in everything, even if I was never fully sure exactly what my part was. Would it be weird to go talk to him? Even if I couldn't say anything, at least I could listen to somebody in the same boat as myself. I don't know. Nobody is really talking about Jessica going away. Oh, I'm sure they are, as people always do, but there is no widespread gossip. Maybe it feels like a dirty thing. God only knows what people are saying, or what rumors were circulating before. If there are any about me, nobody has the guts to tell me.

I had a dream the other night. Jessica was in Nurse Nancy's house. It was just the way I remember it, the half finished art piece with the nails and everything. She kept saying I know you, her face and tone flat. God I hope she's okay out there. I hope she's safe.

Leopold

February 15, 2023

Hello Friends,

Donovan is not doing well, he's basically self-quarantined himself, refusing to leave the house he once shared with Jessica Tran. He refuses to work as well, which is causing quite a stir. The latest Safeway truck has been reportedly delayed by some wintry weather in the Gorge, which always gets people gossiping about freeloaders. Thank god for Jon Seabreeze and his level headedness. Donovan is going through a hard time, as a community we should recognize that and be supportive. Most people seem to be more in that camp, but there's always people who have less empathy. As for me, I've mostly tried to avoid having anything to do with it. All in all, it seems best that I keep my distance and keep my feelings about what happened to myself. There is no use asking questions. There is no use dwelling on what cannot be changed.

I don't want to seem uncaring for writing off the whole thing and my involvement in it. I feel a great mixture of emotions; including guilt, shame, and sadness; but so many other things seem to be crowding in that rather than process it all, I've simply had to abandon it as is and leave it behind. Gary Gunderson has increased the number of people patrolling. There was a small group of Survivors that came near the boundary a few days ago, but we quickly chased them off by yelling threats. To be honest, they mostly just looked cold and hungry to me. Things can't be easy for them I imagine. It's been raining off and on for the past two weeks. People are definitely on edge. When you sit in the warming house you can hear people whispering to each other with concern. Lots about the various evils groups of Survivors have done, or reportedly done, over the years. Also quite a bit about the bastards in the Foster-Powell Neighborhood Association. I've been so focused on the world right around me, first with Jessica, then without her, that I've seemed to have missed the ratcheting up of emotion.

I'm worried about Mom and Charlie. I haven't heard from them in months now. What could be going on over there? Is it just the normal delays, made worse by those bastard fascist Turtles, or is something truly amiss? Even when Mom gets angry with me, I rarely go this long without a letter from her. Just one more thing to add to the bonfire that is my mind. I'm having trouble sleeping at night, so much so that I've taken to volunteering for any job available to try and tire myself out. I've even taken to jogging when there isn't enough to do, something I haven't done recreationally for god only knows how long. I hope you all are safe. I received your last letter, but haven't had time to read it yet.

Cheers,
Leopold

February 20, 2023

Hello Friends,

Well, call it a lesson in human nature, but I think I might have messed up my warming house a bit. Tiring of the few entertainment options available to us, I took it upon myself to expand what we have a bit through some horse trading and various other swapping. Long story short, I managed to convince Janet Hicks of all people to let me borrow her copy of Settlers of Catan. It's in pretty good condition, there's a couple pieces scorched and splattered with wax that must have had a candle dropped on them or something, and there's a couple other pieces replaced by paper cutouts, but overall, not too shabby. You should have seen how excited everyone in the warming house was, even the people who never played the game before. I'm not sure how things are up there, but down here, though we're supposedly living a communal lifestyle, people aren't all that keen on lending out things you can't get anymore. I guess there will always be luxury items, ours have just become very different than they once were.

Anyways, I don't think I would've done it if I had any idea how cutthroat the people in my warming house were. You should have seen the wheeling and dealing going on. It was like watching an old reality show or something. Alliances were created and broken constantly, people were screaming at each other and cursing under their breath, and I thought somebody was going to sweep the table a couple of times. The worst part was when Mr. Robinson managed to get a town built in a space that Deserae Higgins had been shooting for too and he loudly proclaimed the name of his new town as Fuckutopia. Well, Deserae stood up and smacked him in the face. Shocked the hell out of everyone, and then there was all sorts of angry babbling and laughing. It was a crazy thing to see, though not as crazy as the fact that the next night everyone wanted to play again. Maybe I'll volunteer to do night patrols again. I switched over to day patrols about a week ago. Of course if I'm not there to keep an eye on it, Janet will probably insist I return the game, so I'm not sure what to do. Just crazy to see everyone get so cutthroat over a game.

Not much more to talk about I guess. Things are as they are here. I was interested to hear your Collective has grown over the past few months. People crave a sense of community and security I think. It's good to help others, but don't beggar yourselves in the process. We learned that the hard way last winter. You never know when things might get a bit lean.

Your friend,
Leopold

February 25, 2023

Hello Friends,

People are still talking about the damn Survivors, though I have yet to see any in a while beyond a few small groups wandering by no closer than three blocks away or so. I'm not sure what all the hubbub is about. It seems no worse than it was this time last year. Either way, Jon Seabreeze called a meeting so people could talk about it. People are all sorts of worked up, and I don't think Gary Gunderson is helping. He seems to be taking quite a bit of pleasure in whipping a number of people into a bit of a frenzy. God, you should have heard the people standing up to speak. According to them it's only a matter of time until Survivors either bring the virus up from Milwaukie or just cut all our throats in our beds. Don't get me wrong, I don't trust any Survivors one bit, but I haven't seen anything recently worth kicking up this much of a fuss about. Quite a few people also seem pretty convinced that the Foster-Powell Neighborhood Association is looking to screw us over. That at least seems a little more true, a lot of the Survivors I've seen have been wandering around on their side of the line, though that might be more a sign of incompetence than malevolence. I don't know. Smiley Dave Larson tried to raise some of these exact points, but he got shouted down by some of the more verbose. He looked pretty pissed about it. Jon Seabreeze didn't say much during the meeting. He mostly just sat next to his wife. He looks tired.

It's been raining here for about a week. One of those cold ass middle of winter rains that just soaks right through you right down to the bone. I helped unload the latest Safeway truck, and between that and patrolling got rather soaked, so I took today off so I could sit next to the fire and avoid a chill. Mrs. Robinson was telling some pretty good stories about growing up on a dairy farm, but I kind of tuned it out and just stared into the flames in the fireplace. It seemed like a good day for ruminating. I thought about Jessica Tran for a while, then Leslie Hayes, and then even Nurse Nancy for a bit. I wonder how Donovan is doing. He doesn't leave his house much anymore. At some point he's going to have to snap out of it. You can't be able and a freeloader at the same time. What's done is done. Eventually we all have to move forward.

Hope you and Danny are doing well. Stay dry in all this rain. The last thing anybody needs is to catch a chill. The world has enough problems without unnecessarily adding to them.

Cheers,
Leopold

February 26, 2023

Dearest Friends,

Mom and Charlie are dead. A fellow named Sam Cocking who I knew growing up wrote me a letter to let me know. Apparently, they've been dead since last month. It's hard to get many details, a lot of it's been blacked out by the fucking fascists, but it has to have been the virus. What in the hell else would kill somebody so fast? I guess it just goes to show that the Safe Zone isn't worth two shits. Come live under martial law and still die of the virus. What a great combination. I guess I should be glad that I never took Mom up on her constant invitations, you can go with little hassle if you've got immediate family already there, though I kind of wish I had just so I would've had a chance to see them before they went.

Of course, out there was never really my home. Oh sure, I went out there and stayed from time to time, even whole summers back when I was in high school, but it was never really home like down in Canby was. When Mom and Dad got a divorce, and she married Charlie, I never really got the draw of going out to the middle of nowhere, even when Dad died when I was in college and they were all I had left. Don't get me wrong. I loved my Mom, and Charlie was a hell of a nice guy, even if he was a bit of a nut, but they're place was never really my place. Does that make any sense?

I remember the first summer I went out there and Charlie had me driving combine. Good god, I was only fourteen years old, what in the hell could he have been thinking? I don't know. Maybe he was thinking pretty sly. I'd been bitching and moaning about wanting to go back up until that point, but there was too much to think about driving that combine to give me much time for worrying about what I was missing out on back in Canby. Charlie was always a bit of tricky son of a bitch that way. For a guy who never had any kids until I came along, he sure seemed to have things figured out. Even Dad liked Charlie, which given the dynamics of the situation and Dad's general attitude, is pretty damn impressive when you think about it.

I hope they buried them nice, though those fascist Turtles probably just burned the bodies or dumped them in a big hole somewhere. Mom always wanted to be buried up on top of this hill so she could see the mountains. Charlie's opinion was that they might as well just throw his body out to the coyotes so he'd at least be useful in some way. I think I'm supposed to be sadder than I am about this. I just can't seem to draw too much out of the old well these days.

Your friend,
Leopold

March 10, 2023

Hello Friends,

A family came to the boundary two days ago. There were four of them, two parents and two teens. They looked pretty worn out and bedraggled. They said that Survivors had burned their house down. Several patrollers opinioned they were probably Survivors themselves. One of us, Shenoa, said she recognized them as a family that lived south of Woodstock, though she hadn't seen them since before things went to shit. Most people agreed that it wasn't really proof that they weren't Survivors now. We've been hearing that things down in Milwaukie are getting pretty bad virus wise, and the family seemed pretty cagey regarding answering too many questions about what happened, or whether or not any Survivors tried to infect them or anything like that. In the end, Gary Gunderson ordered them to leave. When they got a little argumentative about it, a few people tossed some rocks at them like they were stray dogs or something. I felt kind of bad for them, but I'm not sure what the hell else we could do. They obviously weren't telling the whole truth, and the last thing we need here is a wave of virus.

In other news I've befriended Donovan a bit. Started checking in on him last week and managed to coax him out to walk my patrol rounds with me. It's entirely unnecessary for him to do it, but I think it's probably good for him. He's still pretty mopey, but at least he's mopey outside. I don't know, it's been kind of nice to have somebody to talk with. Old Chuck Henderson used to walk with me from time to time last summer, always claimed he needed to get away from his husband for a bit, but his knee started hurting him so he quit. It was all right by me, I'm not sure why the hell he wanted to talk with me, and all he ever talked about was technical stuff that I wasn't too interested in. He did seem to like my stories about getting out and about, which I guess makes sense given he hasn't left the confines of the Republic since the second wave. Anyways, with Donovan I mostly talk about Mom and Charlie passing, and he mostly talks about Jessica of course, which causes me to bite my lip a lot, but in the end I guess it is what it is.

We heard some dogs barking the other day. I wonder if they're the same ones I heard a couple of months back. Can't imagine there's too many left out there. After all, Survivors and the such still have to eat. Can't imagine it myself, but I'm guessing it all depends on how desperate you get. I hope that family is okay. We did the right thing, but still, one would have to be a cold hearted son of a bitch not to feel some guilt. Anyways, give Danny a big hug for me. One of those super awkward ones where you loop your arms over his shoulder and under his crotch. Danny always hated those.

Yours truly,
Leopold

March 16, 2023

Hello Friends,

Donovan can't seem to shut up about Jessica Tran, though I wish he would. It's grating on me. I feel like I'm stuck in a bad rendition of The Telltale Heart by Edgar Allan Poe. There's a little voice screaming inside of me to just blurt out my part in everything whenever he brings it up, but of course I don't, because that voice is stupid. It constantly tells me to do things that are most definitely not in my best interest. I can remember one time, when I was working on my car, back when cars weren't just hunks of metal outside our houses, I had the engine running and the hood open. The stupid voice just kept telling me to grab the belts. I of course didn't listen then either, but it certainly freaked the shit out of me. Who in the hell has a little voice in their head casually telling them to hurt themselves. I only listened to it once, when I was a kid and Dad left me home alone. I was making some mashed potatoes with an electric handheld mixer, and the voice told me to grab the beaters. It was convinced I could stop them with my bare hands. Well, it was right, because they most certainly did stop when my fingers jammed them up. Luckily they designed those things not to seriously hurt people, but after that I learned to be a lot more careful of that stupid voice. Anyways, I can't tell if I'm letting Donovan walk with me because I enjoy his company or because I feel bad. I'm not going to stop, I just wish he'd start moving on with his life already.

In other news, I had to return Settlers of Catan to Janet Hicks. She never asked for it back, but that's what I told everybody in the warming house. I'm just sick of them fighting about it. People were getting way too crazy, to the point that some people weren't even talking to each other anymore because so and so didn't trade someone else for wood two weeks ago. Just plain ridiculous. We're back to cribbage games and Mrs. Robinson listing the names of all the cats she's ever owned in her life, but everyone being in a sullen silence seems like the better option than people actively screaming at each other.

Anyways, not much else to report. It won't stop raining here. Each day is the same. Gray clouds and drizzle, a good hard pour mid-afternoon, followed by more drizzle. Everything is rather monotonous. Gary Gunderson is still trying to keep us all jacked up about Survivors, but we haven't really seen much and a lot of the people on patrol are starting to talk behind his back a bit. I don't know. Don't really have time for such things. Better close, I'm supposed to help Kaden Ortiz with the stills tomorrow. He's mostly taken it completely over, but still needs my help from time to time. I'm pretty sure Jessica was screwing him too. Sometimes he says things. I don't know. God only knows who's all screwing who.

Leopold

March 23, 2023

Hello Friends,

A group of Essentials came to the boundary the other day on ATVs pulling carts of equipment. Apparently they were scoping sewer lines or something like that, making sure there weren't any major clogs that might cause issues I guess. They had a few pipe junctures within the Republic that they wanted to check out. Gary Gunderson told them no and sent them on their way. Caused a bit of a kerfuffle afterwards. Chuck Henderson especially was pretty pissed about the refusal to, in his words, recognize that the infrastructure currently sustaining us is more delicate than we realize. Gary countered with the fact that the virus is still spreading down in Milwaukie, rumors are ranging from its completely died out to pretty much everyone down there is dead, and that the safety of the community is of the utmost importance. Smiley Dave Larson tried to speak up in Chuck's defense, but people shouted him down. Jon Seabreeze was mostly quiet again. He just doesn't look well. We need him. The meetings are feeling more like shouting matches all the time, and people like Gary and those in charge of other parts of the community are basically running things by edict rather than consensus. I'm not sure why Jon Seabreeze looks so haggard, but I know people have been going to him more and more to settle stupid little disputes or to complain about each other.

I was thinking about Mom and Charlie today when I was doing my patrol. It seems strange to think of them being gone, but in some ways it seems much the same as it did before. After all, aside from the occasional letter, it's been like they were gone for years. I remember Charlie let me have my first beer. I was helping him harvest, and after a long day he opened up the fridge and pulled out two, one for me and one for himself. He said I had put in a man's day so I got to have a man's drink. I felt proud. Mom would have of course been against it, or so I always thought, until I found out that Charlie had discussed it with her earlier. She never said a thing about it. What had that conversation been like? It's such a stupid way to mark one's transition towards adulthood, but it did make me feel something, and I've never forgotten it, so maybe it wasn't so stupid after all. That was always the problem with Charlie, you could never tell with him when something was stupid and when it was brilliant. It all kind of just mashed together. I'm glad Mom found him. I know he made her happy.

Anyways, glad to hear you've all come through the winter with few mishaps. People here are already discussing when we should start planting early vegetables. We've still had frost some mornings, but as always there's a contingent that wants to get started as soon as possible. Just one more dispute.

Leopold

March 29, 2023

Hello Friends,

This damn rain is still falling, and to be frank I'm already quite sick of it though god only knows how many more months we're going to have of this bullshit. Patrols are so miserable that even Donovan has quit walking with me most of the time. On the one hand I'm sorry to have lost the company, but on the other, he still can't stop going on and on about Jessica. It's like that time Danny went to Sweden and just watched Black Panther over and over again. You remember, he watched it like four times. Who watches a movie that many times on a single flight?!

Anyways, outside of Donovan and this god forsaken rain, I guess things have been mostly okay. It might be wet, but things are starting to warm up a bit. Fewer and fewer people are spending time in the warming houses anymore, which is probably for the best. People were obviously starting to get on each others' nerves and verbal altercations were not uncommon. I just don't think people do well cooped up together for that long. I don't know. It didn't seem that bad last year. Maybe people are just getting more comfortable with the world we live in now, less willing to put in that extra effort to be civil because it's an extraordinary situation.

One of the rainwater tanks we put in last summer collapsed. It was one of the hot tubs. Nobody is exactly sure what happened. People just found a big divot in the ground over the top of it, so it's pretty obvious that the top collapsed, but why or how is really a mystery. Some people are convinced that a group of Survivors snuck in and somehow did it, which makes absolutely zero sense to me, but you know how people get when things happen. Most likely we screwed up building it, overestimated how much weight the top could bear, and it's just been building up to collapsing over time, but of course that's not near as satisfying or interesting of an explanation. Either way, a group of us have started digging so we can try to set it back up and get it right this time. We'll probably have to check out all the other cobbled together rainwater tanks as well. Thank goodness they're just an experiment right now and we don't actually need the water they store, but still, we need to be prepared. It's as Jon Seabreeze always says, things are going to keep eroding, so we damn well better be ready.

On a more positive note, Joanna Seabreeze and the gardening council have directed people to start planting, so people are starting to get busy again. Maybe we'll get off our asses and get started on some other projects as well, such as tearing up the pavement for more farm ground. It's normal for things to slow down during the winter, but this year seemed much more so than last year. It's a little frustrating for those of us who consider ourselves doers.

Leopold

April 7, 2023

I went to Mrs. Robinson's to help hang some shelves this
morning. Apparently Mr. Robinson has carpal tunnel or
something like that and has trouble using tools. I was glad to do
it. I've been trying to do as much as possible for other people
whenever possible. I don't know what went wrong. She wanted
them high up on the wall, and the brackets had to be moved to
match the studs, and that was a whole thing, and then Mr.
Robinson couldn't hold his end level while I was trying to juggle
my end and the tools. Then when I finally got a screw in, I was
horrified to find that I had missed the stud all together. We tried
two more times, but for the life of me I couldn't find the stud,
and both the wall and shelf looked like shit, and I just sat there,
feeling worthless, and that's when Mrs. Robinson said: "it's all
right we'll figure something out." I hated her tone. It was the
tone of her being mad at how badly I had screwed up, but instead
of just saying it, she tried to be polite while still using a tone that
said everything. I apologized, and then had to leave before I
punched a wall or something. I went and lay on my bed for
about an hour, gazing up and imagining designs in my ceiling.

I feel so impotent of late. The entire world seems to be swirling
down the drain around me, and there is not a damn thing I can do
about it. I can't even hang a god damn shelf apparently. I don't
feel like a man. I feel like a little boy stuck in a chaotic world,
doing nothing but hoping the adults figure things out. It's
maddening. It wasn't always this way. At least I don't think it
was, though maybe I'm just imagining otherwise. I know I felt
this way during the first and second waves, during the riots.
Watching the whole world split apart and knowing there is not a

goddamn thing you can do about it. I can remember going to some of the protests, the peaceful ones, it felt like the right thing to do at the time. At first it was about something grander than ourselves, something to help those truly in need, but then things began to turn violent. The Essentials got scared and cracked down. The second wave began, the protests were no longer about what they were originally about. Riots became the norm. The Turtles came to town. Things escalated. People were beaten bloody. More people came out. More and more people got sick. What was the point of any of it? What kind of beasts were we? Jumping from emotional outburst to emotional outburst, failing to do anything but scream out our frustrations at a world out of our control. Have we learned anything? Are we any different now?

I can't remember the last time somebody asked me if I was all right and actually wanted an answer. I keep telling people everything is going to be all right, but there is nobody to do it for me. All I want to do is lay my head down on somebody's lap, have them stroke my hair, and tell me everything is going to be all right.

Leopold

April 11, 2023

Hello friends,

Somebody lit an abandoned house on fire two nights ago, just on the east side of 52nd on the southeast portion of the boundary. I was maybe only five blocks away when I saw the flames. I started yelling and hollering and ran down to try to put it out. At first, I went inside, thinking that maybe I could put it out before it got too big, but it was already up into the ceiling so I got the hell out of there. People came down with hoses and we started spraying water on the houses around it to keep them from going up too. There was only so much we could do with garden hoses. The hydrants still work, but we don't have hoses for them. Thank god it's been a rainy bitch of late, I would hate to think of something like this happening in the middle of August. I'd hate to see us end up like Brentwood. Anyways, a number of us were up most of the night and a good part of a day manning the hoses. The last of the hot spots weren't put out until the afternoon. I would've written you sooner, but I was so tired that I went straight to bed and slept for twelve hours or more.

Gary Gunderson was of course all sorts of up in arms about the whole thing. He's pretty damn sure it was Survivors, got all sorts of people worked up about it. Smiley Dave Larson isn't so sure, but not a lot of people seem too keen on listening to an answer that involves not knowing. Personally, what I saw when I went in the house looked like a couple of candles knocked over on some blankets. Made me think more of a little love nest than some hardcore Survivors looking to cause problems. However, I've not told many people about it. People don't really seem too interested in narratives other than their own anymore. I don't really feel like getting in a fight. This whole day has been nothing but Survivors this and Foster-Powell that. Who knows. I saw a small group of Survivors three nights ago. They made a bit of a fuss and yelled at us for a bit, but not much else. I don't think the winter was very easy on them by the look of things. I wish Jon Seabreeze would speak up some more, but he doesn't seem too interested. He doesn't seem to leave his house all that often. I hope he isn't sick or something. Joanna Seabreeze seems as chipper as ever, helping with the planting of new gardens.

To add further woes, it was discovered that some of the vegetables we canned last fall apparently didn't seal right. A number of jars went bad and will have to be thrown out. We of course still have the Safeway trucks coming regularly, so food isn't a problem, but it's a blow because we all know we can't depend on them forever. No one is sure whether it was defective lids or just human related screw ups. Either way, it did little to improve on the general mood.

Your friend,
Leopold

April 15, 2023

Hello Friends,

I read your last letter with a great deal of interest, especially the portion about the decision to make your Collective of Burning Creek more into a mutual defense pact than an actual functioning society. I don't want to sound judgmental, but I hope me relaying some of the issues here at the Republic have not dissuaded you from following a similar path. There are of course going to be growing pains, especially as the old world completes its collapse into oblivion, but it does not mean that the foundation is not strong. For all of our problems, I still fervently believe that what we have here is better than anything the old world offered. Yes, people are still people, with all of their foibles and ignorances, but at least now everybody has a place. There is no homelessness in the Republic, no poverty, none of the old biases, and everyone contributes as they can to the mutual progress forward. There is no society in history that hasn't had to weather storms that challenged its ideals, and we are no different. We will emerge, stronger than before, better and more solid for having faced such challenges. I disagree with people, and at times even doubt their good intentions, but I still believe fervently in the institutions and beliefs upon which the Republic of 47th and Long was founded.

The past few days have been sunny and warm, with soft spring breezes kissing the cheeks of our emerging inhabitants, making their way out into the world again to plant our gardens, repair our houses, and take on whatever tasks need to be done. It was such a beautiful day that I took it off to relax and read. This morning I went on a run to burn off some energy, the first time I've done so in quite awhile. As I jogged the grid of streets that has become my world, I remembered jogging back when the second wave was just getting started. People had started blocking off sidewalks with trash cans and other such things. People were just beginning to become wary of each other and the growing risks. How much the world has changed since then. Those of us who could change with it were the bright ones. Those who refused remain unhappy in this new world.

I wonder what Nurse Nancy would think of this world we've created if she could see it? Would she still be as stubborn as ever, insisting that it was her duty to go to the hospital each day, ignoring the risks to the rest of us? I must admit that I've been thinking of her again of late. Perhaps we could've been kinder to the Essentials, but perhaps they could've been more willing to listen to reason as well. It does not matter. It's in the past now, and we must move forward to the future.

Cheers,
Leopold

April 21, 2023

Hello Friends,

I've been enjoying the strange spate of warm weather we have had over the past few days. I think there is nothing more perfect than a warm spring day, things just cool enough where you feel the need to wear a jacket. I wonder what we're going to do as our clothes further degrade? A lot of what people are wearing is beginning to look rather ragged, and handwashing only does so much to keep things clean. It's strange the things you don't really think about when it comes to self-sufficiency. I doubt we could grow cotton here, even if we could get our hands on the right seeds. Perhaps we could get our hands on some sheep or something. I imagine we'll all increasingly look rather like patchwork quilts moving forward.

I think the vibes here in the Republic are improving somewhat with the nicer weather, or perhaps I've just quit paying attention. Either way, I think everyone having something to do again is certainly helping. Most of the focus has been on planting and tending this year's gardens, plus various other tasks meant to aid us in being more self-sufficient. I've been mostly helping dig out a root cellar to better store various vegetables throughout the year. Patrolling was getting a little old and Kaden Ortiz really doesn't need my help with the stills anymore. Sweating a bit has felt pretty good. There's nothing quite like physical labor to improve one's outlook on life.

I broke the rules a few nights ago. I'm not sure I should even tell you about it. There's a few rumors circulating that Gary

Gunderson is reading people's mail before it leaves. It sounds
like total bullshit to me, the usual crap that circulates its way
through tight knit communities, though it is a little alarming how
many people would apparently be okay with it if he was.
Anyways, I snuck out past the patrols and wandered around a bit.
It was strange to be out alone beyond the boundary. Several of
the houses are still inhabited, though even less than last year I
imagine. Fewer and fewer people want to be alone anymore.
There's safety in numbers. I had to hide a bit when I got too
close to Reed College and a patrol of Warrenites came past. I'm
not sure exactly where their boundary begins. I've heard rumors
that there are a few smaller groups coalescing here and there in
the area, but I didn't see any sign of patrols or anything like that.
A lot of the houses are abandoned, though it's a bit hard to tell
the difference given how they're all dark. Maybe the Republic
could scavenge some of them for materials. It would help to
have more building materials, and it would probably cut down
on the number of Survivors in the area.

Hope you both are staying well. Sounds like the outbreak in
Milwaukie has cooled down.

Cheers,
Leopold

May 2, 2023

Hello Friends,

Things have gone crazy here unfortunately. A group of Survivors attacked early this morning. They lit a few fires near the southern boundary to act as a distraction and then a group raced out of the Foster-Powell Neighborhood Association on bikes, chucking rocks at windows and even throwing a few Molotov cocktails as they went. They were a horrible sight to see. There were probably about fifty or sixty of them all together, spreading out as they went like ink spilled across a page, screaming as they came. Most had some kind of improvised weapon which they swung with wild abandon, seeming more inclined to cause random damage rather than actually going after anything specific. A group did break into one of the houses used for food stores, grabbing as much as they could as quickly as possible, smashing mason jars that they left behind.

There were some people out in the early morning hours working in the gardens, mostly Boomers. The Survivors fell on them with wild abandon, taking them to the ground and forcefully spitting in their mouths, laughing as they screeched how one can't be sure whether or not they have it. God only knows how many are Mary's. One of the people caught was Joann Seabreeze. They left her badly bruised amongst a row of tomatoes, her face covered in their vile spit. All will have to go into quarantine, as will any who got close enough to care for them.

We rushed to intercept them, but they were too quick. Too many people hid in their houses rather than come out to help. Too many people were tied up in trying to keep the fires under control, everything unusually dry for this time of year. Smiley Dave Larson managed to shove a stick into the spokes of one of the Survivor's bikes, sending the bastard flipping over his handlebars. I've never imagined Smiley Dave could be so enraged. He had an aluminum baseball bat, and he just kept hitting the Survivor in the head again and again, a metallic ping sounding with every stroke. He swung until the man's head was nothing but a bloody smear. None of us dared go near him. His entire front was covered in blood. When he could finally swing no more, he let the bat drop, and stood there, gazing at all of us around him, tears pouring down his cheeks. He then meekly let himself be led away to be put into quarantine. We burned the body where it lay, covering it with old blankets and kerosene. The smell was horrific.

My god what has happened? The whole attack was all in only five to ten minutes. People cluster together now, talking in hushed tones, some moving from group to group while others give the dead eye to those who were the more vocal about doubts that the Survivors would attack. The world has changed. I'm frightened.

Leopold

May 3, 2023

Hello Friends,

The world truly and fully has gone to shit. The Survivor attack
has pushed people over the edge. Turmoil below the surface has
at last boiled over. There are no more respected voices of reason
in the crowd, at least none willing to speak up. Jon Seabreeze
voluntarily went into quarantine to be with his wife. Smiley
Dave Larson is in quarantine too, though even if he wasn't I
doubt he'd be much good to anyone. Beating that Survivor to
death has made him almost entirely catatonic. God only knows
what kind of shit got unzipped with such an experience.

People are blaming the Foster-Powell Neighborhood Association
for the attack, and Gary Gunderson has done little to help the
situation. In fact, he has whipped it into a frenzy. The foolish
ass. I don't think he's fully realized what he's released. People
were whispering all day, coalescing into larger groups, then
people began yelling, screaming for justice, and then they were
on the move. There were maybe two hundred of them all
together. Many had hammers and other such tools. Some had
guns. They crossed 52nd and started beating on everything.
Some people lit fires. I followed behind, not wishing to
participate with such insanity, but unable to not watch. Foster-
Powell did not suffer the excursion without striking back. A
large group of them came down the street, yelling and waving in
the air whatever weapons they could lay hands on. The two
crowds faced off, spitting and screaming vile curses at each
other. It reminded me of two bros at a bar, their shirts off,
circling each other, beating their chests, trying to get the other to

throw the first punch. People started throwing rocks and other such things. A few people on both sides went down, heads bloody. Individuals began creeping closer, self-appointed champions wailing on each other as the crowds cheered and booed. You could feel it building. You could feel what was coming. Several people began shooting guns into the air, but when it had little effect they lowered their aim and started shooting into the crowds. People on both sides panicked and ran, it was hell to see. Several people were trampled. We all rushed back to the safety of the Republic, but as soon as we got across 52nd we turned and held our ground. The Foster-Powell bastards refused to cross the street.

People split off and went home throughout the night. Gary got the patrol folks organized and ready in case of an attack. By daylight they were the main group still waiting, which appears to be the same on the other side. It was strange to see the smoke rising so close in the golds of the sunrise. Something has broken, and I don't know if it can ever be fixed again. I feel sick to my stomach.

Your friend,
Leopold

May 5, 2023

Hello Friends,

Hopefully these letters will get to you eventually, but I'm not sure if they ever will. I've taken to carrying them with me at all times, in case something happens. The past two days have only seen things escalate somehow even more. Two nights ago several houses on the other side of the boundary went up in flames. There's a lot of confusion over who was responsible. Some people claim it was people from the Republic, some that it was Survivors, and some even claimed that the Foster-Powell bastards did it themselves to give them a reason to attack us. If the last is the case, they certainly failed to take advantage of it, but Gary Gunderson certainly did not. By morning, a group of people I used to patrol with were in solid control of an area east of 52nd several blocks down Steele. However, it did not last long, by midday a big group of heavily armed Foster-Powell folks came at them from three sides. There were gunshots. None of ours were hit, but I've heard a couple of the Foster-Powell people went down. Either way, by the end of the day 52nd was the boundary once again.

I wish I could say the next day was better, but it would be a lie. There were no grand skirmishes as the day before, but instead people on both sides pushing every car they could find to make barriers, dodging random potshots, some from guns, but most from various slingshots, both old store bought and homemade. One of ours got hit, a shot right to the head. A man named Jaeger who was often a block or two ahead of me when walking patrol. Nothing much was done for him. He was just wrapped in a sheet and thrown in a shallow hole down in Woodstock Park to be out of the way.

I don't want much to do with any of it. What kind of insanity has gripped us all? How in the hell does any of this make a damn bit of sense? I wish I could talk to Jon Seabreeze about it, or even Smiley Dave Larson, but Gary Gunderson has made it very apparent that nobody is to bother those in quarantine. He's got a few people keeping an eye on things. At the very least I've managed to avoid being involved in the fighting, though a lot of the people have called me a coward to my face, especially those I used to patrol with. I did help push the cars to the boundary. Thank god things in the Republic are relatively flat. I'd hate to have had to help push any of them uphill. I was maybe a block away when Jaeger got hit. A bunch of us ran down to help, but others yelled at us to scatter, bellowing that clumping only made people easier to hit. What the hell is going on? Nothing makes sense right now. I think others feel the same, but I don't dare talk about how I feel. So many people are being swept along. A disturbing number of people are all in, openly declaring it's about damn time.

Leopold

May 8, 2023

Hello Friends,

I'm not sure why I'm writing to you today since nothing much has changed. Perhaps just to remind myself that I am indeed alive. The mail carriers haven't come and I see no hope of them coming anytime soon, so maybe you won't even ever get these letters. I don't know. Maybe I just need something to do that feels normal. I spend most of my time in my house anymore, though sometimes I come out to help in the gardens. There's not much happening on the boundary. Mostly just people staring at each other from behind rows of cars, some smaller ones tipped up on their sides, yelling the occasional curse at each other and hucking the occasional rock. It's a weird little sideshow, with some people over there every day, and others just going every now and again, almost recreationally. You know, after a tough day, go down to the barricade, toss a couple rocks at strangers, get a good night's rest. The usual. Sometimes I hear a gunshot or two, but it's pretty rare. Nobody wants to waste the ammunition needlessly.

I tried to go see Jon Seabreeze today, but two of my old patrol buddies were outside, keeping people away. According to them he doesn't want to be disturbed. All sorts of rumors are swirling, but the main story going about is that Joanna Seabreeze is pretty sick. I can't really imagine one without the other. Maybe he can't imagine it either. I did manage to speak to Smiley Dave Larson a bit through the window of the quarantine house he's in, but he didn't have much to say. Smiley Dave never did some of the things a lot of us did back in the early days. Back when I could feel the fervor boiling its way through my blood, when I was willing to do what needed to be done without question. He's a gentle soul, Smiley Dave, and I don't think he'll ever really recover. This is less than optimal given it leaves us with just Gary Gunderson, who's been strutting around like a damn rooster. When I was a kid, Charlie and Mom had a rooster that always went at you whenever you went up to the henhouse. Had to carry a bat with me when I collected eggs. At times I'd like to take a bat to Gary. Probably won't though.

I wish there was something more I could do or say, but I doubt I'm in the majority. People still flinch when they hear gunshots, or when someone needs some medical care because a rock got them, but overall everyone seems to have accepted all of this as normal. It doesn't feel like things used to, back when the People's Republic of 47th and Long really meant something. We had a dream, a vision of something better, but I'm having a hard time seeing how what we have now is any better. People seem to be the same as they've always been. Gary claims we must go through the fire like tempered steel. I don't have a god damn clue what he's talking about. I hope you and Danny are well.

Leopold

May 12, 2023

Hello Cynthia,

The Essential postal service was re-established yesterday. Gary Gunderson didn't want to let them in, but for most people it was a step too far, and he was forced to give in. I'm so very sorry to hear about the loss of Danny. He was a good man. Maybe one of the best of people. There are so many things I wish I could express right now, but mostly I wish that I could be there for you. I wish I could hold you so that we could cry together until the world ends. So many people have lost loved ones, so many who were the best amongst us have gone, but I never thought Danny would be amongst them. He always seemed invincible. No matter what the world threw at him he always had a cocky grin, as though he knew that the story was about him, and therefore he'd always make it through.

He was always better than me. From the first day we all met in that running group up on Mount Tabor I knew he was better than me in every way. Everyone liked him. He didn't even need to talk to people for them to like him. I can remember him swaggering about, happily gazing out at the world, secure in his knowledge that it was a good place full of good people. To be honest, I never could figure out why he wanted to be my friend, and now he's gone, and I still don't know, and I never will.

Danny was always willing to give a helping hand. I shouldn't really be surprised that he would step in to protect someone, even if that someone was a Survivor. Crowds are fickle things. They build momentum and can avalanche out of control. I know

I could never do what he did. I know I could never step forward and declare that no, what's happening is wrong. In the end we're all animals, though animals that can remember and regret. When I think about what happened to Danny, I feel ashamed, as though I was the one who put the knife into his gut. Forgive them Cynthia. Please forgive them, even though what they have done is unforgivable. There is so much of this world that is driven by fear. There are so many mistakes we all wish could be undone. It is horrifying what we can do when surrounded by others.

If only more of the world was like Danny. If only more of us could find it in ourselves to do the right thing without hesitation or doubt. If only more of us found ways to be less scared. I wish I was there with you now. I wish I could've stood next to Danny to protect someone whose only sin was a past affliction and a hunger in their belly. I wish I could've been there with both of you through the good times. I wish I could roll the whole world back to what it once was. I wish.

With deepest sympathies,
Leopold

May 19, 2023

Dear Cynthia,

I don't know if you should bother trying to answer this letter, because I can't guarantee that I'll be here if you send one. It has all become far too much, and the world grows heavier by the day. Joanna Seabreeze died around six days ago, or at least that's the best estimate of those who found her. Jon Seabreeze is gone. Nobody knows where. The only reason they finally got brave enough to check was because nobody was taking the plates of food left on the front steps for them. Nobody seems really sure how many days it took for anyone to get brave. Without Jon and Joanna our little experiment seems over. What have we really built if it cannot outlast its founder? Smiley Dave Larson is officially out of quarantine, but he rarely leaves his house. He seems broken. Maybe that's what people say about me.

Things have only escalated here over the past week. Old Chuck Henderson designed a rudimentary catapult which some of ours used to throw flaming bits of this and that nearly a block into Foster-Powell. Chuck thinks with some tweaks he can get it to fire multiple blocks. The Foster-Powell folks of course weren't very happy about this. A few nights ago they tried an attack to destroy the catapult. They were thrown back, but two of ours got killed in the resulting melee. Janet Hicks of all people spoke up about this, claiming we were needlessly escalating. I thought about speaking up with her, but before I could, she got into a yelling match with a few folks that got out of hand. They knocked her down and started kicking her. One of them was Mrs. Robinson. They probably would've killed her if Gary

Gunderson hadn't shot his gun into the air, though not soon enough to save her face from looking like hamburger. What's happened to us? What have we become?

I've been volunteering to patrol on the west side, as far away from the barricade as possible. I was scared that if I kept avoiding helping that bad things might happen. I know people have been talking about me behind my back. Saying things. Everyone needs to be helping. There's no room for anything else. It makes me sick. After all I've done for this place. My hands never feel clean, yet now I'm nothing. When we first started this place, we had all sorts of grand ideas. No more hierarchies, no more biases, no more -isms of any kind, no more any of it. People still say such things, but it all sounds so empty. Just magic words they wrap themselves with so that any action becomes okay, as long as they can somehow tie it to gaining or saving the dream. I saw Leslie Hayes in a dream last night. She was hanging from the tree where they found her, cackling at all of us. Insisting she was the only one amongst us truly free. Strangely enough it didn't frighten me. She's right.

Leopold

May 23, 2023

Dear Cynthia,

I couldn't go through with it. I made all the preparations, and even went down into the darkness with my rope, to the very tree Leslie Hayes chose. I tied the closest approximation to a noose I could manage and threw it over a branch. I stood there in the darkness and stared at it, but I could get myself to go no further. Do I have a strong will to live, or am I just a coward? I kept thinking about Nurse Nancy looking up at me with her tired beautiful blue eyes, down on the floor where Gary Gunderson had thrown her. He was yelling at her. Asking her if she understood what he was saying to her. Demanding that she acknowledge him, but she didn't look at him. No, she just stared up at me with her tired eyes, her beautiful bright blue eyes, her face completely devoid of emotion. When she spoke, the words were for me, her tone almost neutral, as though none of it really mattered, a monotone simply stating a fact. I know you, she said. I know you. Then we started kicking her. I'm not sure who started, I'm sure it wasn't me, but whomever it was I followed with all the rest. We kept kicking and kicking. She didn't make a sound beyond the grunts of the air leaving her lungs. She didn't cry out or beg. She just kept watching us, her gaze boring through the goggles and masks which hid our features, until finally I had to close my eyes, but even then, I didn't stop. None of us stopped until Gary Gunderson ordered us to stop, and then I went into a backroom to puke, and it was there I saw the mosaic of the horse made out of nails. We set fire to the house with her inside of it, or at least what used to be her. We removed what we had done from the world. I would like to claim it was the only time I was involved in such things, but it would be a lie. We told ourselves we were doing what had to be done. We told ourselves we were the good guys, and that those against us were bad. It's okay when you're the good guys. You can make anything okay when you're the good guys, people boiled down into binary caricatures. Is there anyway to be forgiven for such things? Could you ever forgive me? If I made my way north to you, would you welcome me with open arms? I don't know if I would welcome myself. I wish I was more like Danny. I wish we could all be more like Danny. I don't know what to do. I don't know how to feel. I don't know anything. I can't undo what I've done, and I can't unknow what I know. I wish I was stronger. I wish I was able to do what needs to be done. I don't deserve pity or anything like it. I'm a coward. I'm a sheep. I'm a fool. I know you, she said. Was it her way of asking me not to do it, or did she know that I was a weak person, and was simply stating a fact? When the world was normal, whenever I crossed the street, I'd try to meet the gaze of drivers. So they'd always remember me if they hit me with their cars I used to joke. They say the best jokes always have a kernel of truth to them. I know you, she said. Did she see the same thing I did when she said it? Did she see us at the Goodfoot? Did she hear the funk music? I don't know.

Leopold

June 5, 2023

Dear Cynthia,

Given the lack of letters, I doubt you really want to hear much from me. Given what I've done and how Danny died, I can't say that I blame you. I'm still here at the People's Republic. I'm too much of a coward to go anywhere else. I'll admit that I've thought about it. Maybe I could go down to Gladstone, or perhaps further east into the Numbers. I've heard there are groups out in the Numbers, though most are doing their best to survive under the idea that someday soon there will be a vaccine available. Maybe I could even go further east, out to Gresham where the Essentials come from. Can one become an Essential? What's the outside world like? I'll admit, aside from a few instances where I've had to, I haven't really thought much about it in a long time. Maybe someday there will be a vaccine. For the first time in a long time, I hope that maybe there is one someday.

The Republic and the Foster-Powell Neighborhood Association are still sniping at each other. The Foster-Powell folks have built their own catapult, and both are flinging things at each other, mostly things that burn. Most of the houses right along 52nd anymore have at least some scorch marks on them, or so I've been told. I don't go around there if I can help it. All of it seems more like background noise anymore, though it's having an effect on many things. The vegetable gardens do not look as good this year. If we get half of what we got last year I'd be surprised. I worry about the Safeway trucks. We'll need them all the more if the gardens don't produce, and god only knows how long it will be until one side or the other tries to keep the other from having access. I worry about it, or something with the water pipes, or a fire getting out of hand. I worry a lot anymore, but I don't really seem to have it in me to do any more than worry. Part of me I think would welcome it.

I've been walking patrols at night, but only along the western boundary. Things have changed since all the bullshit started. It's lonely walking by myself all night, but I don't really want anyone walking with me. Donovan took a rock to the face about two weeks ago. It was a big bastard. Cracked his skull. Died of an infection a few days ago. I wonder if he ever got over Jessica leaving. I hadn't really talked to him in a while. Guess we'll never know. I think if I could do patrols with anyone, I would want to do them with Danny right now. He'd have something clever to say that would make everything seem better. Maybe after we got done, we'd sit up on the roof, sipping beers and watching the sunrise, just like we all used to do. That would be nice.

Yours Truly,
Leopold

June 20, 2023

Hello Cynthia,

I hope this letter finds you well. I'm guessing given you never responded to my last letter, that you won't respond to this one either. I wish it was different, but I understand. I should probably stop writing to you, but in some ways these letters are all I have. I'm sorry that I keep sending them even though you obviously don't want to receive them. I don't know why I'm still writing. I keep to myself mostly anymore, and so have little to tell you even if you did want to hear it.

There was a big fire about two weeks ago on both sides of 52nd. Several blocks went up before people got things under control. It's been hot as hell lately, and it seems like everything is ready to go up without much reason. I think the fire scared everyone on both sides. They've quit firing the catapults of late and most of the altercations along the barricades are verbal rather than physical. Maybe things will start to calm down a little bit. I don't know. Maybe not.

Somebody cut down the Japanese maple outside the Seabreeze household. Nobody has any idea who did it, but it seems right given they are no longer here. Sometimes I wonder what happened to Jon Seabreeze. Did he just have enough, decide it was time to go, or is he dead and buried somewhere? Who knows. Eventually I guess I'll stop asking the question of what happened, much as with Jessica Tran. All sorts of people were upset about the maple getting cut down. Gary Gunderson is fully in charge now. I don't think he has any trees in his yard.

I've been thinking about the big bike ride I took early on, the one to downtown back when I was sent out on scouting missions. Jon Seabreeze always made a habit of seeing people off back then. He had that winning smile of his, and he told me what I was doing was important for the Republic. Jon was always good at those little speeches. He had a way of making you feel like you were a part of something important. One might have been a little cog, but they were a respected little cog. I don't think I have it in me to do something like that again. What would I do if I left? Nothing is certain, but other things are more uncertain than others. I don't have it in me to handle that kind of uncertainty. I don't think I'm tough enough to be out on my own.

I was thinking about Danny again when I was walking last night. Do you remember that time he got so drunk he thought my computer chair was a toilet? Silly bastard. Funny how our favorite memories always involve someone being ridiculous. Perhaps ridiculous is just more genuine.

Your friend always,
Leopold

June 29, 2023

Dear Cynthia,

I know I promised that I'd quit writing, but here I am again. I imagine by now that you're not even opening these letters, in which case, I'm truly writing them purely for me. Who knows, perhaps soon I'll just write them and never send them. It would likely be better that way. At least then I wouldn't be harassing you. I don't know. Somehow there is still a small part of me hoping that you're still reading these letters. Hoping there is still a part of you that gives a damn about what happens to me. Things here are about the same as they have been, though perhaps that's mostly because I don't do much beyond the bare minimum to ensure I earn my meals. I certainly don't do much with regards to socializing.

There were rumors a few days ago that Jon Seabreeze was seen out in the Numbers, somewhere out by Powell Butte. Apparently there's a collective or something out there which lets new people join, and one mail carrier who knew our mail carrier thought a guy he saw there looked an awful lot like Jon Seabreeze. Who knows. It doesn't really matter as far as I can tell. The world is as it is, and Jon Seabreeze being alive somewhere else has little to do with life here. I don't know, maybe it's true. It's kind of nice thinking about him out there, living his own life. Maybe Jessica Tran is with him, and as long as I'm trying to make myself feel something positive, I might as well imagine Nurse Nancy is there as well.

The nights have been warm here, not really cooling off much. It feels more like mid-August than late June. I wonder what's happening with climate change anymore. Has all that has happened made it better, or is it all somehow worse? I have a hard time seeing how it could be worse, but you never know. I imagine it will take some time to notice a difference. Either way, it's about as important as wondering whether or not Jon Seabreeze might be out by Powell Butte. I exist. I lack the wherewithal to change my existence or end it, so none of these things have any bearing on me moving forward. In some ways it's kind of freeing, to feel nothing, to have no passions and no fears. When one is ambivalent about their own existence, but yet continues to exist, it is a level of peace beyond contentment. I think contentment requires a conscious decision to feel contentment. I am mostly numb, which requires no thought at all. I am not the person who did those terrible things before, and I'm not a person who may do better things in the future. I am simply a collection of atoms, filling a purpose and taking up space. I do not have to worry about it being enough, for I'm no longer measuring anymore.

Your Truly,
Leopold

July 17, 2023

Hello Cynthia,

I promised myself that if I did not hear from you by mid-July that I would quit writing, and now here we are and I find myself writing this one last letter. It is the last I promise. One must atone for their sins, and if losing you is part of my atonement, then it is something that I must accept. I hope someday when you think back about me, that you think of the good parts of me as well as the bad, for we are all complex people, neither righteous nor evil, though some of us fall further to one side of the spectrum than the other.

There is not much to say about life in the People's Republic of 47th and Long. There was a good sized fire a week and a half ago which burned several blocks in the northwest corner. No one is sure who or what started it, but of course the rumor mill is ripe with theories, with Gary Gunderson as always pushing that it was Foster-Powell. There will be violence again. Many households have become empty, people disappearing in hopes of finding someplace less chaotic. I can only hope them the best. I was here in the beginning, and I will see it through to the end.

When doing my patrol last evening, with the sun setting beautifully over the hills with their broken radio and cell towers, I saw a skinny man dressed in rags two blocks away. We stood and stared at each for a moment. It's the first real human connection I've felt with someone for awhile. Without thinking I raised my arm in greeting, and though in halting herky jerky movements, as though unsure, he did the same. I will admit that it nearly brought tears to my eyes. I do not know who he is, though I imagine he is likely a Survivor. He had the look about him, but I no longer see them as monsters, but rather just faulted human beings much like the rest of us. People doing their best to navigate and survive the chaos of our world. I've a strange thought in my head, which unlike other thoughts I actually plan to carry through into reality. The Survivor looked hungry. Tomorrow I will gather some food and leave it outside the boundary for him. Perhaps I will do it again the following evening. Perhaps eventually I will stay near the food, and we can talk, as strangers used to talk before. Perhaps we can learn not to be afraid of each other. Perhaps I will offer my hand to him, and perhaps he will take it. Perhaps with these few simple human gestures, we can make things better. I don't know. People would say I'm crazy if I told them such things. I would be even more shunned than I already am. But I know I'm safe telling you, and perhaps that's all I need.

Take care of yourself my friend. May you see the world bloom again as it does in our dreams.

Lovingly yours,
Leopold

Also Written By The Author

The Uncanny Valley

We all know a Paul. A person who seems to see stuff that isn't there. The type the polite call quirky and the blunt call nuts. Conspiracies? He's got a few. He's got his finger on how the world really works. He knows what kind of shit is coming down the pipe. Flee across the West Texas desert to Mexico? Makes sense to him. Feel like you're being watched? You bet your ass someone is watching. Best turn off your cellphone. Troubles? Of course, that's just part of life. Doubts? No time for doubts. Shit is getting real. Get in, buckle up, crack open a beer. The only real question is, how far down the rabbit hole are you willing to follow?

An Unsated Thirst

They say that an author's first stories are their most raw. Here is a collection of S.W. Campbell's first short stories and writings. Combining both published and unpublished works, An Unsated Thirst explores victory and defeat, triumph and shame, and an unflinching view of our naked selves. How one views such stories is dependent upon the mood of the reader. Whether we are at our highs or at our lows. However, it is hard for any of us to claim that such stories are ones that we cannot identify with. Contained within these pages are parts of our lives which we try to forget, though they are an important part of what makes us whole. Such stories should be embraced, accepted within ourselves so we can better accept them with others.

Papaya

When a devastating hurricane hits the CAribbean island of Domenique, its inhabitants are forced into a singular struggle to survive and rebuild. Isolated in their midst is Ted, a Peace Corps volunteer who fled the ashes of his former life only to find himself labeled an outsider. Infatuated by the enigmatic wife of his only friend, Ted thrusts himself into a world beyond his comprehension. As obsession turns to desperation, tensions grow and Ted is forced to decide exactly how far he will go to rebuild amidst the muddy ruins.

Stumptown

There are places where people say things are better. Where the downtowns do not empty after dark and people dare to dream beyond their means. Quirky utopias where the sins of the past are washed away by gentle rains and we all go forward arm in arm together into the brightening sunshine. Distant locations flocked to by young pilgrims, unencumbered by the deeply driven roots of age, where everything will be different. Combining both published and unpublished work, *Stumptown* is a collection of stories about ordinary people, navigating their personal anxieties and drama in a time when uncertainties were still tucked away and not allowed to distort the sense of hope in the air. It is a soliloquy to naivete, and the belief that a better world is a place rather than an idea.

More information can be found at:

www.shawnwcampbell.com

About The Author

S.W. Campbell was born in Eastern Oregon in 1983 after a harrowing drive through a fog. He currently resides in Portland, Oregon where he works as an economist and lives with a lovely house plant named Morton. He has had several short stories published in various literary reviews, some of which appear in this work, and has also self-published several books. His work can be found at www.shawnwcampbell.com.